STAR TREK
PRODIGY™

SUPERNOVA

Written by Robb Pearlman

Based on the television series created
by Kevin & Dan Hageman

Based on *Star Trek* created by Gene Roddenberry

Based on the game *Star Trek: Prodigy – Supernova*

D1508957

Simon Spotlight
New York London Toronto Sydney New Delhi

SIMON SPOTLIGHT
An imprint of Simon & Schuster Children's Publishing Division
1230 Avenue of the Americas, New York, New York 10020
This Simon Spotlight paperback edition January 2023
TM & © 2023 CBS Studios Inc. Star Trek and all related marks and logos are trademarks of CBS Studios Inc. All Rights Reserved. Nickelodeon and all related marks and logos are trademarks of Viacom International Inc.
All rights reserved, including the right of reproduction in whole or in part in any form.
SIMON SPOTLIGHT and colophon are registered trademarks of Simon & Schuster, Inc.
For information about special discounts for bulk purchases, please contact Simon & Schuster Special Sales at 1-866-506-1949 or business@simonandschuster.com.
Cover art by Alecia Doyley
Book designed by Kayla Wasil
The text of this book was set in Basic Sans Alt.
Manufactured in the United States of America 1222 OFF
10 9 8 7 6 5 4 3 2 1
ISBN 978-1-6659-2543-3 (hc)
ISBN 978-1-6659-2542-6 (pbk)

CHAPTER ONE

It was morning on the Federation starship USS *Protostar*. At least, Dal *thought* it was morning. Or, more to the point, he *hoped* it was morning. It was kind of hard to tell what time it was in space without looking at the ship's chronometer. And as helpful as Hologram Janeway was, even Dal recognized how annoying it would be if he'd kept asking her what time it was all sleepless night long.

He'd hardly slept, because every time Dal closed his eyes, he remembered. He remembered how, just a short time ago, he and the rest of the *Protostar*'s crew had been prisoners of the Diviner on Tars Lamora. How the pain from the Watchers' weapons would hurt his body, and how the pain of feeling completely and totally alone, despite being surrounded by hundreds of other Unwanted, would hurt his spirit. Dal tried wrapping himself in his blanket and focusing on the good things that had happened, like finding the Federation starship in which he was now flying through space. How he and his crew joined together to not only escape Tars Lamora, but also to return to that distant planet and liberate the rest of the Unwanted from the Diviner. How happy a little doll created from spare parts could make Gwyn.

But no amount of blanket wrapping could ease his mind. Neither could counting something called sheep or drinking replicated cups of warm milk (both of which, Janeway insisted, were tried-and-true tricks Earthlings used to get to sleep). So every time Dal closed his eyes, he felt like he was immediately transported, hungry, back to the mines of Tars Lamora. Or helpless beneath the cilium tendrils on that M-Class Murder Planet in the Hirogen System that had tried to eat them all. Or stuck in a cage, even just a few days ago in the marketplace on Odaru.

Dal couldn't stop thinking about how they had narrowly escaped with the necessary material to repair the *Protostar*'s transporter system. As much as Dal remembered—and tried to forget—how he'd felt in the past, he also couldn't stop himself from thinking that any amount of hunger or helplessness or fear was worse now because he was not alone. He cared about his crew. Dal was the captain and understood that he had to maintain a brave face for them. If he was brave, they would be brave.

After what seemed like days of just lying there, Dal threw off his blankets, rubbed his eyes, and swung his legs off the side of his bed. "Computer, lights," he said, and his cabin was illuminated in the warm glow of a simulated sunrise. Dal surveyed the room and stepped onto the cold floor, which shocked his bare feet so much, he had to hop around until he found his boots. Starfleet boots were a lot more comfortable than the footwear he had to wear as a prisoner. *Shinier, too,* thought Dal. *Being a captain sure has its perks! And,* he silently admitted, *its responsibilities.*

So it was morning on the USS *Protostar*. Well, it probably was.

And Captain Dal R'El was on duty.

CHAPTER TWO

Dal walked onto the bridge to find Hologram Janeway. Intended as an ETH, an Emergency Training Hologram, to aid and advise the Starfleet-trained personnel that were supposed to be occupying the *Protostar*, this lifelike computer-generated replica of the real Kathryn Janeway was, once again, helping to get a crew back to the safety and security of Starfleet.

Janeway stood, at ease, beside the captain's chair. *Dal's* captain's chair. As much as Dal understood that the *Protostar* was, technically, the property of Starfleet, the ship had quickly become his home, or at least his home away from home—wherever his real home was. And until the ship was returned to Starfleet, Dal had no problem claiming it, and the captain's chair, for himself. And yet, even after all these weeks, Dal still had trouble believing where he was. The sleek lines and temperature-controlled comfort of the *Protostar*'s bridge were a far cry from the rough-hewn, broiling-hot mines of Tars Lamora. The gleaming utilitarian silver and gray of the circular bridge were warmed by the view seen through the massive bank of almost-floor-to-ceiling windows lining its front third.

"Good morning, Dal," said Janeway.

"Morning, Janeway," said Dal, sliding into the seat. *His* seat.

"Morning?" asked Janeway.

"It is morning, isn't it?" Dal searched the bridge for the closest chronometer. Janeway lifted her hologram mug of coffee to her lips and smiled. "Oh, it *is* morning, Dal," she said, pausing to sip, "but from the looks of you, I'd agree it's probably not a good one for you. At all."

"Ohhh. Do I look that bad?" asked Dal, leaning toward his boot to inspect his own purple reflection in its shine. Janeway herself never looked anything but pristine and Starfleet-manual ready. Her official uniform, a black jumpsuit with maroon shoulders, fit perfectly over her gray shirt. The shine of her gold combadge paled only in comparison to her wit and intellect. Dal's confidence in himself was matched only by his respect for his holographic adviser. As captain of the *Protostar*, Dal's was the final word. But that didn't mean that he couldn't take her suggestions and ideas under advisement.

Janeway leaned in. "I wouldn't say you look bad, Dal, but you do have more rings beneath your eyes than Saturn has around its middle. Did you get any sleep at all? Did you record your captain's log yet?"

Dal turned and, in a clumsy effort to change the subject, busied himself by pushing some colorful spots on the console embedded in the arm of the chair. "I got enough. Don't worry about me! I'm just fine. Looking good and captaining like any captain would captain! I'll do the log later. It's too early to log." Dal wondered if the *Protostar*'s life-support systems kept track of his resting and waking hours. Could it tell when he was sleeping? Could it monitor things like respiration or heartbeats? Would Janeway call his bluff and check?

"You're the captain," said Janeway.

Phew, thought Dal as he alternated between reading the same flashing notices on his personal operations station and trying to tame the gray and white hair that stuck up in all directions from the top of his head. Somewhere between decks, the lights in a Jefferies Tube were flashing on and off. From the controls on the captain's chair, Dal tried to fix the issue. Janeway's programming allowed for Starfleet personnel, especially those still learning, to test and find their own limits. She was confident, based on the crew's performance thus far, that they would continue to grow, even if part of that growth was learning how to fail. But, just in case, she ran a diagnostic to make sure the lights in the tube were on when Dal was finished messing around.

The doors at the back of the bridge swooshed open as Jankom Pog, the ship's engineer, walked in.

"Jankom Pog loves breakfast food," he said. "If only I could have breakfast food all day long. Wait—could I? Did Jankom Pog just invent a new thing?"

Zero floated in behind him. "I do not think so, Jankom," they said, taking their place at the helm.

"Whadda you know about eating, Zero?" asked Jankom, stuffing the last replicated Delvan fluff pastry into his mouth. "You're noncorporeal—you have no mouth to eat with!"

"That is true," Zero agreed, tapping the area on their metal containment suit where their mouth would be, "but that doesn't mean I haven't heard of the ancient Earth tradition sometimes described by the acronym 'ADB.'"

"'ADB'?" asked Dal. "What's 'ADB'?"

"Ac-ro-nym? What's an acronym?" asked Jankom.

"An acronym is an abbreviation of an idea or concept, using the first letters of each word in a phrase. In this case, 'ADB' stands for All-Day Breakfast. During ADB, families and friends gather for lunch or dinner, but prepare and consume food that would normally be served during the morning repast."

Jankom was astounded. "Is that ... can it be true, Janeway?"

"It is, but I usually keep to just coffee in the morning," she said, taking yet another sip of her seemingly bottomless mug. "And in the evening."

"I meant, is that what 'acronym' means?" clarified Jankom. "But Jankom is glad to have all the information so he can ask for ADB at any time of day. Or night!"

Once again, the doors to the bridge swooshed

open, revealing the rest of the *Protostar*'s crew—Gwyn, Rok-Tahk, and Murf.

"Brrrrrblpthhhhlsllllll," greeted Murf.

"I think Murf means 'Good morning,'" said Rok-Tahk merrily, "but he did say the same thing when I accidentally stepped on him yesterday, so who knows."

"Jankom made that sound after too much gagh once," said Jankom, spinning around in his chair. The rest of the crew decided to not ask questions.

"Ooookay," Rok-Tahk said, trying to move the conversation along. "Where are we off to today?"

Dal straightened in his seat. "I think we'll still go, um . . . that way," he said, pointing directly ahead.

"Oh, so the way we've been going?" asked Rok-Tahk.

"Yep. That's the way to Starfleet, so that's the way we'll go!" Dal replied confidently.

"Brrrrrblpthhhhlsllllll," said Murf. Again.

Gwyn stood silently beside Zero at their navigation station and stared thoughtfully out the windows that took up the bow of the *Protostar*'s bridge. She traced the gold fretwork on her arm. It looked like an intricate piece of jewelry, but this fretwork was not mere decoration. It was a Vau N'Akat heirloom given to her by her father. She could control it with her mind and shape it into any configuration. Gwyn often absentmindedly touched her heirloom when she was deep in thought.

Gwyn was not, and would probably never be, known as "a morning person." She awoke each day not with Rok-Tahk's boundless optimism, or even Jankom's insatiable hunger, but with the lingering, biting memories of mornings on Tars Lamora. It was in those early hours, sometimes even before she had a chance to wipe the sleep from her eyes, when Drednok, her father's attendant, would give her a list of orders for the day. Her entire day would be laid out for her. Days filled with trading bars of chimerium with Kazon for new Unwanted. Days spent spying on miners, translating, squashing uprisings, and figuring out ways to manage some sort of independence with Drednok's glowing red eyes constantly watching her. All the while wondering what her father's ultimate plan was, and whether she was right to help him. Gwyn's father was known to her and to everyone on Tars Lamora as the Diviner. She was his progeny, and he was ruthless in trying to train her to fight. And how to kneel. Drednok sensed that Gwyn questioned her father's motives, and made it very clear to her, whenever he could, that she would be wise to not overstep her boundaries. He made his distrust of Gwyn known to the Diviner.

It was difficult to make out a lot of details of the stars and planets that whizzed by at warp speed, but she was able to discern enough to know that the crew was hurtling through space at what would have been an unthought-of velocity just a few weeks ago. And some of the twinkling stars reminded her of the shimmers she saw in the eyes of the last Unwanted she bartered for. A young Caitian female whose eyes, like those of most of the young prisoners forced to work in the mines beneath the planet's surface, would probably never sparkle in the sun again. She was proud of herself and the rest of the crew that they had recently returned to Tars Lamora to free the Unwanted, but Gwyn had spent far too many mornings in dread to ever say, let alone think, *Good morning.*

Gwyn had so desperately wanted to see the stars for so long that she was rarely able to turn away from them these days. And now here, on the bridge of the *Protostar*, far away from the yoke of the Diviner and Drednok, and surrounded by the safety and support of a crew—of friends—she was able to just . . . look at them. She found herself absentmindedly stroking the nest of fine, dead filament that made up the hair of the doll she'd picked up in the marketplace on Odaru. Since that adventure, Gwyn had kept the doll close to her at all times. She looked at it, a hodgepodge of old starship parts clothed in a dress made of silk scraps, and thought of that young Caitian. Had she ever had a doll like this? Had any of the Unwanted? Gwyn could not recall.

Gwyn raised the doll to her own face. It cast a shadow as they flew by a bright star, surely serving as a sun around which a planet or planets orbited. Its light, and the light of her friends and crewmates, warmed her more than the sun above Tars Lamora ever had.

"Gwyn," said Zero, shaking her out of her fog of memory. "There is something engraved on the foot of your doll."

CHAPTER THREE

"There is?" Gwyn asked, lifting the doll higher.

Gwyn had been so enamored with the doll, especially the way it made her feel, that she failed to notice all its details. *Not noticing details can get a person killed,* she thought, remembering her training. *I won't let that happen again.*

Sure enough, on the bottom of what approximated the doll's left foot, a series of symbols stretched from the doll's heel to its toes.

"What do you think it means?" she asked.

"Maybe it's the code to a safe filled with chimerium?" offered Jankom Pog.

"Maybe it's the name of whoever owned the doll first," said Rok-Tahk shyly. "I know if I ever had a doll, I'd put my name on it so everyone knew it was mine. And they could get it back to me if I ever lost it. But I'd never lose a doll as nice as that one. Never!"

Gwyn smiled at her friend. She sometimes forgot that though her Brikar crewmate was covered with pink rocklike skin, was almost double her height, and many times her weight, she was still an eight-year-old girl. An eight-year-old girl who had probably also never owned a doll of her own.

"Could be, could be," said Dal, stroking his chin. "But maybe it's... nothing? Could it just be nothing?"

Janeway approached the doll to inspect it for herself. "It could be nothing," she said, "but in my experience, nothing is rarely nothing. And sometimes, most times, nothing is most definitely something."

"Okay," said Dal dismissively, "so it's something. Maybe."

"Maybe we should run the symbols through the ship's computers to decipher it?" Zero suggested.

Jankom threw his cybernetic multi-mitt off his right wrist and halfway across the bridge onto the doll, snatching it from Gwyn's hands quicker than she could react. "That's just asking for trouble and

Jankom is not asking for trouble. Jankom's never asking for trouble and Jankom doesn't think any of you should be asking for it either. Haven't we had enough trouble? We should get rid of *this* trouble right now.

"Murf!" he shouted, retracting his cybernetic appendage and sprinting toward the only being on the *Protostar* who could eat more than Jankom. "It's time for more breakfast!"

Murf's smiling mouth opened with a *"Squeeee!"*

As Jankom ran toward Murf's widening mouth, Rok-Tahk swooped the doll up and out of Jankom Pog's grip and held it high above her head. "But if it belongs to someone, we should return it. They're probably worried sick!"

Gwyn extended the gold fretwork from her arm, catching the doll's braids and took the doll from Rok-Tahk's grip. She held it tightly in both hands. "We should figure out what it says before making any decisions."

Dal looked at Gwyn. "You're the communications expert, Gwyn. Can't you read it?"

"It's not like anything I've ever seen, Dal," said Gwyn. "And besides, I'm a little better with speaking languages than reading them. I think Janeway should take a crack at it."

Dal could tell Gwyn, always the overachiever, was disappointed in herself. "That's okay," he said. "I can't do either. What about you, Zero? Can you get anything from it? Maybe it's got some sort of mindy feely mumbo googly woobly? Or something?"

Zero slowly floated toward their young Vau N'Akat crewmate and the doll she held in her hands. "I only know what some of your words mean, Dal, but if you are asking whether or not the doll contains any sort of residual psychic energy, I am afraid I cannot say with any certainty. Medusans are telepathic, but we are not all-knowing."

"Jankom only knows what some of those words mean," said the engineer, slumping in his seat.

"Captain," said Janeway, "maybe I can decipher it?"

"I think," Zero said, "that this doll meant something to someone. It may indeed still mean something." They offered the arms of their containment suit to Gwyn, who gently handed them the doll. Holding it as if it were a baby, Zero floated over to Janeway.

"With your permission, Captain?" Janeway asked.

The crew looked at Dal for a response.

"Sure!" said Dal. "Maybe you can tell us what we're looking at."

Janeway bent to get a better look at the engraving. "It's coordinates."

"Coordinates? To where?" asked Dal.

Janeway stood at attention. "I'm gathering information from the *Protostar*'s Starfleet navigation archives now. Ah, here we are. It's coordinates, all right. Sending to viewscreen."

The giant real-time relay of the *Protostar*'s forward view was suddenly replaced with a static image of three planets of approximately the same size orbiting a star.

"I'm a little behind in my astrometrics, Janeway," said Dal, slowly approaching the image. "What are we looking at?"

With a wave of Janeway's hand, the three planets extended holographically out of the viewscreen. The star situated itself right above Dal's chair, while the three planets began to orbit the perimeter of the bridge. "This is relatively uncharted space. Starfleet's archives indicate that any information they have on these coordinates was relayed by long-range scanners, so there isn't much to go on," explained Janeway. "The only thing we do know for sure is that it's only about a day away at Warp Four."

Zero handed the doll to Rok-Tahk and tapped on their data console. The holographic map zoomed out to include Odaru, the planet they'd just left. "And we could surmise, based on proximity, that it would be entirely feasible that an object that originated at these coordinates, such as this doll, could have made its way to Odaru easily enough."

"So the code is really not someone's name," said Rok-Tahk. The small doll looked even smaller when cradled in her massive arms. "I guess the doll didn't mean something to someone."

"But it *is* coordinates," said Gwyn, "to an entire planetary system, so maybe it means something to a lot of people."

"But what could mean the same thing to so many people?" asked Rok-Tahk.

"Could be a warning. It's definitely a warning," said Jankom.

"Or it could be a call for help," offered Zero. "We are too far away for me to sense anything from those planets, but the fact that the coordinates were inscribed on a child's toy does infer that whatever the owner wanted to convey was a message that affected generations of beings. Including children."

Rok protectively tightened her hold on the doll. "Maybe we can get Starfleet to help? They'd know what to do. Janeway?"

Janeway looked kindly at Rok-Tahk. "We're still too far out of Federation space to contact Starfleet, Rok. And even if they could get our message, they wouldn't be able to get here for weeks, or longer."

"It could be a trap," said Gwyn. "I mean, putting coordinates on a child's toy? That's exactly the kind of thing the Kazon or any of the other traffickers would have pulled to trick and trap other children." Gwyn thought of all the young Unwanted who were brought to Tars Lamora. The Caitian child. Even the rest of the crew.

She tried to do her best. Although she herself was manipulated and lied to, she knew that she was responsible for so much suffering. "It could be a trap," she repeated.

"Oh, it's *definitely* a trap," Jankom agreed.

"But," Gwyn continued, her neuroflux involuntarily

glowing, preparing her fretwork for a fight, "it's worth the risk if we can help children. Or anyone who might be in trouble."

Zero readied their mechanical appendages above their navigation console. "Dal? What do you think?"

What do I think? thought Dal, looking into the eyes of each of his crewmates. *What do I think? I think this could totally be a trap. It's probably a trap. I also think we just set everyone on Tars Lamora free, so maybe we can do it again. And if we can do that, doesn't that make it worth it? Isn't that what Starfleet would want? Isn't helping, doing good deeds—or at least trying to—what Starfleet is about? But I think Jankom has a point. I think we can't help anyone unless we help ourselves. I think Rok is terrified. I think Gwyn's not thinking things through, which is really my thing. Would this be just another way to put my crew— my friends—in danger? Would it delay us too much or put us too far off course? I think … I think … I think …*

"I think, Zero," said Dal, "you need to plug those coordinates in and get us on our way."

CHAPTER FOUR

As Janeway had predicted, it took the *Protostar* almost exactly one day to arrive at the coordinates inscribed on the doll's foot. And as Dal had predicted, he spent yet another mostly sleepless night reliving his past and fearing the immediate future.

Rok-Tahk, Gwyn, Murf, and Jankom Pog joined Zero, Dal, and Janeway on the bridge as the *Protostar* slowed from Warp 4 to half impulse speed.

"We've arrived, Captain," said Zero.

Dal tilted his head as he looked out the window. "That looks . . . different than I thought it would," he said. "Zero, can you magnify what we're looking at?"

Zero touched a button on their console that

turned the clear windows into a viewscreen. The star system was magnified several hundred times. As Dal had suspected, the *Protostar*'s visual sensors were picking up a very different view than anyone had expected. The ordinary star (in as much as anything in an anomaly-filled galaxy was ever ordinary) was enveloped by an enormous object, keeping most of its light and warmth away from the three planets in orbit around it.

"I've never seen anything like this," said Zero.

"Me either," said Janeway.

Dal sat back in his chair, trying to comprehend what he was looking at. "Janeway? What is this? Where'd the star go?"

"I'm running some sensor scans and it's definitely still there, Dal," said Janeway, "but it looks like the sunstar is almost completely encompassed by a Dyson sphere."

"Why would anyone want to wrap up a sunstar?" asked Dal.

"For the same reason our ship has a gravimetric protostar containment system," said Rok-Tahk. "Power."

Jankom Pog slowly approached the viewscreen.

"Protostars are baby stars that give off baby power. That's a grown-up sunstar. It gives off a lot of power."

"I know a lot about containment fields," said Zero, tapping the top of their own. "So what now?"

Dal straightened up in his chair and tried to look decisive. "Well, I guess we should go explore, right? I mean that's what Starfleet would do. Suit up, everyone!"

"If I may, Captain," interjected Janeway. "You might want to first scan the area for signs of any abnormal radiation or other anomalies."

"Yes, right," agreed Dal.

"And then maybe scan the planets for life signs?" she continued.

"Okay. That's good." Dal leaned in expecting more. "What else?"

"Well, I don't want to tell you what to do . . . ," Janeway replied.

"Tell him!" exclaimed Jankom.

"Just tell me," Dal quietly agreed.

"Well, then, depending on whether or not we find any life signs, you might want to open your hailing frequencies to initiate contact and prepare to beam down to the surface of one of the planets."

The crew looked at Dal.

"Yes! Yes, do all that—do what she said!" said Dal.

The crew got to work following orders. Jankom initiated the scans for life signs, while Gwyn opened a communications channel.

Trying multiple frequencies, she repeated, "This is the USS *Protostar*. We've come to return something that belongs to you. Please acknowledge." Gwyn spoke in multiple languages, too, hoping the inhabitants of one or all three planets would understand what she was saying directly or through the *Protostar*'s internal universal translator. She also hoped they'd be friendly.

"No life signs from the planets," reported Jankom.

Zero set the ship into a final stationary position several hundred kilometers away from the closest planet. They initiated long-range scans to make sure the *Protostar* would be out of the direct path of any asteroids or debris that might be headed their way and, to be thorough, a scan to make sure nothing was going to come up at them from the planets. "Long-range scans show nothing coming our way. But ... this is curious. I am picking up some energy signatures from various points on all three of the planets. Some of them look like generators of some kind. I can't quite tell what the others are yet. I'll continue to monitor."

Rok-Tahk ran a quick diagnostic to make sure the coil they'd just repaired in the *Protostar*'s transporter system was still holding and functioning at maximum efficiency. Seeing that everything was in working order, she scanned the planets to make sure they were safe to beam down to. *Breathable air, that's good. Seems a little chilly, but nothing our thermally regulated Starfleet uniforms can't handle. Hmm, those look like good spots—flat terrain.* "I can beam us straight down to any of the planets' surfaces from here on the bridge, Dal," she said. "Jankom and I refitted our combadges to allow for site-to-site transport, so we won't have to go all the way to the transporter room."

"Jankom did most of the work," Jankom said, before seeing Rok-Tahk put her hands on her hips, a silent suggestion that he admit that that wasn't the entire truth. "Well, Jankom did most of the helping."

"Sounds good, Rok," said Dal. "Why don't you plug in the coordinates for all three planets now and keep them on standby. Once we get all the data back, we'll pick the best one."

Rok-Tahk smiled. She was always happy when her brains were recognized over her brawn. "Aye, Captain!" she replied, inputting all the information into the *Protostar's* transporter systems. With nothing else to do, Rok-Tahk turned her attention to running routine diagnostics.

Hmm, she thought, *looks like one of the replicators went offline. Jankom probably asked for too many of those Delvan fluff pastries again. That's an easy fix.* She delicately placed her large finger on the display, and felt a slight vibration emanating from the control panel.

The vibration became a tremor and grew to a rumble.

"Anyone else feeling that?" she asked.

Suddenly, before anyone could answer, the ship tilted violently to the left, throwing its crew to the ground.

"What was that?" asked Jankom from beneath a console.

Dal climbed back into the captain's chair. "Janeway, what was that? Run a—" But before he was able to finish his order, Rok-Tahk noticed that the transporters were suddenly online, and milliseconds away from beaming them off the bridge. Before anyone could do or say anything, the bridge was shocked by an overwhelming and blinding flash of light.

And then, everything went black.

CHAPTER FIVE

Dal opened his eyes. His head hurt, and the dim light that was coming from above stung his eyes. *Great, another sleepless night,* he thought, reaching down for his blanket. *I really thought I'd shut off the overhead light before I went to bed.* Unable to find his blanket, he came to the slow, head-pained realization that he was not waking up in bed. The light he saw was not coming from above his bed, but from the Dyson sphere–enveloped sunstar that he was now seeing from the surface of a planet. He quickly stood and, gasping for breath, felt around his body to make sure he was all there and in one piece. *All limbs accounted for,* he thought, feeling his nose, ears, and even the tail that emerged from the back of his head. He took a deep breath. *Air seems* *okay too.* Wrapping his arms around himself for comfort, Dal looked around the dimly lit terrain to get his bearings.

"Hello?" he asked the nothingness around him. "Hello? I'm not sure where I am?" Nothing.

Dal tapped his combadge. "Dal to *Protostar.*"

He tapped again. "Dal to Janeway."

"Dal to . . . anyone?" Each call was met with ever-growing silence. Dal took the combadge off his chest. The faint light from the sun barely shone against it, but Dal could see enough to know it at least looked intact and functional.

Panic suddenly gripped Dal's throat. *Where is everybody?*

"Hello! Hello?!" he yelled again, louder than before. Dal remembered he had his tricorder. He hoped that would work, even if his combadge wouldn't. Maybe Starfleet tech could do a better job figuring things out than Dal's own eyes and ears. *It's possible,* he thought, and he began to scan his immediate surroundings.

As his tricorder beeped, indicating a nearby life-form, Dal heard a faint, somewhat familiar murmur coming from just a few meters away. "Ugnnnnhhhh."

Following his tricorder's directions, and running in the direction of the sound, he stopped just before tripping over Gwyn. The metallic ornaments in her braids and her fretwork reflected just enough starlight for Dal to see her lying prone on the ground. She was as groggy as Dal had been and seemed more than a little surprised to find that her fretwork had been extended, like a blade, in front of her. Had whatever just happened to them kicked in her defensive impulses? Her offensive ones?

Dal helped her to her feet as she tried to get her eyes accustomed to the planet's low light. "What . . . what happened?" she asked.

"Dunno," Dal admitted. "But whatever happened fried my combadge. I can't contact the *Protostar*, Janeway, or anybody."

Gwyn tapped the Starfleet symbol on her chest. "Gwyn to *Protostar*. Janeway, can you hear me? Zero? Zero, please respond. Gwyn to Jankom. Rok?"

The crewmates looked at each other. "Murf?"

Dal raised an eyebrow.

"Well, it was worth a shot," Gwyn said. "You and I are able to communicate without me having to speak your language, so that means the combadges' universal translators are still working. They're not broken. At least not totally. Maybe there's something in the atmosphere of this planet that's inhibiting comms, or the *Protostar*'s communication systems are down. Unless…"

"Unless what?" asked Dal.

Gwyn wrapped her psychically controlled fretwork back around her arm where she usually kept it. "Unless . . . the *Protostar*'s been destroyed and there are no comms left. No anything left."

Dal couldn't believe what he was hearing. "Wait, wait, wait. What are you talking about? Why would you even—"

"I'm just being realistic, Dal. Terrible things happen all the time." Gwyn looked at the horizon. "All. The. Time. The only thing we can do is prepare as much as we can and then deal with it. As best as we can."

Dal placed himself between Gwyn and the horizon. "Okay, first of all, can you please just for once, just for now, give your dark and broody thing a rest? It's dark and broody enough here. Second, you're forgetting that I was the one who got us all off Tars Lamora, so I'm kind of an expert at getting off planets. How could you forget that? It *just* happened! Unless you're not forgetting it and intentionally leaving it out, which is really taking the dark and broody thing to a new level. So let me remind you, either way: You do dark and broody. I do daring escapes from inhospitable worlds. And third..."

Gwyn waited. "Third? What's third?"

"They're third," said Dal, pointing behind her.

It took a moment for Gwyn to process what she was seeing.

"Are those...?" Dal asked.

Gwyn's face hardened to a grimace as her fretwork extended back into a blade.

"Watchers."

CHAPTER SIX

*D*al couldn't believe his eyes. Or Gwyn's confirmation. The Watchers, the mechanical insectoid guards that tormented him and the other Unwanted on Tars Lamora, were somehow here on this planet. And headed their way.

Though they could barely hear their telltale robotic chirping, Dal and Gwyn could certainly see their glowing red eyes as each of their four legs brought them scuttling closer.

"But how?" Dal asked, seemingly frozen in place. "Weren't they all deactivated!?"

Gwyn knew there was a time for questions and a time for action. This was definitely the latter. There was no time for them to consult their tricorders for information on the unfamiliar topography surrounding them.

"We have to run," she said. "Now!"

Dal listened to his friend, and the two took off as quickly as their humanoid legs could take them. Dal gasped for breath. The air was breathable, but his lungs still weren't used to atmospheres that weren't as polluted as Tars Lamora's. As he furiously pumped his arms, he could feel the shoulder seam of his uniform rub against a years-old scar. It was the first place he'd suffered the sting of a Watcher's energy bolt. And though the mark on his shoulder had healed over the pain of his skin, it still hurt as much in his memory. Somehow, the Watchers had known that his manacles hadn't actually malfunctioned on their own accord. So they punished him for damaging the equipment, for trying to escape, for taking time away from mining, and as a deterrent for future insubordination. He would never, could never, forget how much it hurt— how much they had hurt him.

And now, despite the fact that they were off Tars Lamora, that Drednok and the Diviner were no longer holding them prisoner, and that their mechanical minions were offline and destroyed, here the Watchers were. And getting closer. He turned to Gwyn for explanation.

Gwyn scanned the area around them for points of tactical advantage. And as if their impending threat wasn't enough, memories of the Watchers flooded her mind too. As her father's progeny, she'd never felt under direct threat from the Watchers, but that didn't mean she wasn't keenly aware of the damage they could do. She'd borne witness to countless instances of the pain the Watchers could inflict. And now here she was, no longer under the protection of the Diviner, no longer able to work the system to neutralize Drednok's threats. She'd been unable to help any of the Unwanted in the past. But she'd do whatever she could, however she could, to help Dal, and herself, now.

"Dal!" screamed Gwyn. "Look over there." Dal turned to see a small outcropping of rocks. Though it was hard to make out the details in the dim light, it did seem big enough for them to hide behind. Dal nodded and followed Gwyn in the direction of safety.

A few moments later Dal peeked out from behind the rock. The Watchers had stopped their march toward them and were scanning in multiple directions.

Amazingly, the rocks they found themselves behind were blocking the Watchers' scans. They had some time to assess the situation.

"The Diviner must have found us," Gwyn whispered, more to herself than Dal.

"But your father is dead."

Gwyn flinched at being reminded she was her father's daughter. "Maybe not. I survived seeing Zero in their true form. Even if I lost my mind."

"You only lost some of your memories, not your mind, Gwyn. And they'll come back."

"I hope you're right, Dal."

"If your father is alive, we can't let his evil bots find us. Or use us to steal the *Protostar*. If they do, we'll all be dead."

"We need to keep running." Gwyn pointed to a small hill.

The friends bolted away from the safety of the rocks toward the hill. Suddenly, the sand beneath their feet began to vibrate. They slowed to regain their balance but were thrown to the ground as the vibrations grew stronger. The ground began to pulsate beneath them as a tidal wave of sand and dirt rose before them. One final *thud* opened a wound in the ground, releasing a torrent of Watchers up into the eternally twilight sky. They soared above Dal and Gwyn in a wave, obscuring the dim sunstar. Their evil red eyes fixed on the duo lying on the ground. As they began their descent, the Watchers readied their scorpion-like tails for a full assault.

"There are too many of them," Dal screamed.

Gwyn readied her fretwork for battle. "There always are."

As the first Watcher made its way to the ground, Gwyn pierced its mechanical shell with her fretwork saber. Somersaulting and kicking it off, Gwyn sent it careening into one that was a second away from hitting Dal from behind. They clamored together and exploded in midair, pieces flying everywhere.

"Here!" yelled Gwyn. She tossed Dal a leg and a tail that had landed near her.

"What should I do with these?" he asked.

"Fight!"

Dal held the discarded Watcher leg in one hand while he swung the tail above his head. He stabbed a Watcher right in its red eye. Hopping up and over its prone body, he used the tail to rip open the underside of another that was coming at him from above. *These things really come in handy,* he thought. *I wish I had had them on Tars.*

While Dal used the remnant Watcher parts to destroy more Watchers, Gwyn put her fretwork and fighting skills to work. She'd always hoped that the years spent training under the uncompromising and cruel eyes of Drednok and the Diviner would lead to doing something more than keeping the Unwanted in line. Sidestepping a series of energy blasts, she somersaulted toward a grouping of rocks. She picked them up and, with pinpoint accuracy, threw them at just the right places on the Watchers' visual sensors and mechanical outer casings. Watchers watched, they didn't listen, and they certainly didn't feel, so Gwyn felt no guilt for coming at the now-blinded mechanical insectoids and driving her fretwork through their cores.

Dal watched as Gwyn continued to telekinetically morph her fretwork into a series of weapons and protective shields, taking down most of the first battalion of Watchers.

"That. Was. Amazing!" he exclaimed, throwing his weapons to the ground.

Gwyn allowed herself to smile as she tried to

catch her breath. "Thanks." She compared her pile of Watchers to the small handful in front of Dal. "You . . . did okay too."

"I did!" Dal said, pleased with himself.

"We don't have a lot of time, Dal. Watchers come in waves and that was just the first one. We must find a place to hide and regroup. Try to figure out what's happening."

Dal and Gwyn climbed over and around the bodies of the Watchers. One dim red eye flickered back to life. Gwyn ran it through with her fretwork.

After about fifteen minutes of walking, they could start to hear the clicking of more Watchers coming from just beyond a ridge. The friends took off running, directionless, away from the sound. As they made it past an empty riverbed, Dal saw a hole in the ground. *Probably an abandoned well,* he thought as he pushed Gwyn into it. And immediately lost sight of her.

And then, before he knew what was happening, he lost sight of everything aboveground.

CHAPTER SEVEN

"Ugh," moaned Dal. "On the ground again?"

"You're not on the ground! You landed on me!" exclaimed Gwyn, throwing him off her. "Why did you push me? What were you thinking would happen next?"

"I didn't think much past hiding in the hole." He looked up at the underside of the ground around the hole they'd fallen through. The remains of an old staircase snaked down from the hole to the floor. Broken doors lay at its bottom. "Is this a cave?" asked Dal.

Gwyn activated her tricorder. "Looks like it. From what I can tell, there's a huge network of tunnels stretching on and on in every direction. Just like the ones on Tars Lamora."

Dal recoiled at the comparison. "Hopefully *not* just like the ones on Tars Lamora."

Gwyn had to agree. "Tricorder readings are showing a life sign down here. Just one. But past that, an enormous energy source. I wonder if that's what's keeping us from communicating with the *Protostar*?"

"I wonder if that life sign is friendly or not," said Dal.

"Well, those Watchers are going to be here any second. We may not be able to outrun them, but we can try to slow them down. We'll deal with the life sign when we get to it."

"Leave it to me," said Dal, picking up a rock and aiming it at a precariously balanced bit of dirt and rocks hanging from around the hole they'd fallen through.

"What are you—"

Gwyn couldn't finish asking her question before Dal threw the rock up, dislodging some dirt and ground from the ceiling near the entrance. At first a few pebbles and dust started to fall. But before long, larger chunks started to rain down.

"You caused a cave-in!" Gwyn shouted, grabbing

Dal's hand and running deeper into the tunnel.

Dal followed her lead into the darkness. "That was the plan!"

Gwyn couldn't believe how reckless Dal could sometimes be. She stopped and released his hand. "That was a bad plan! What if it all came crashing down on us?"

Dal's self-satisfaction continued unabated. "I, um, didn't think that far ahead?"

Gwyn turned and leaned against the wall of the tunnel. *As usual,* she thought.

Once they were confident the rest of the underground ceiling wouldn't come crashing down on them, the crewmates backtracked to inspect the newly formed barrier. They agreed that no air or light, let alone a Watcher, could make it through.

"Come on," said Gwyn. It would take her a little while to get over Dal's impetuousness. *But,* she had to admit—at least to herself—*it did work. If only he'd stop smiling about it.*

The crewmates started back on their way through the complex network of tunnels. Taking their tricorders' directions, they made what seemed to be hundreds of left and right turns, sometimes climbing over the debris left from other partial cave-ins. They came to a dead end.

Dal inspected the wall. "Nothing short of a Xindi jackhammer is gonna break through that."

Gwyn agreed. "I wish Rok were here. She has two Xindi jackhammers for arms."

"C'mon," Dal said, "the clock's ticking."

They backtracked. Each step took them closer to the mysterious life sign and the power source. Eventually, they found themselves in a similar but larger antechamber than the one they'd fallen into. They'd both spent enough time in the mines of Tars Lamora to recognize that this one felt less organic than the other one—more intentionally constructed. There were too many right angles, too many smooth surfaces, and too few variations in the strata for any of it to be naturally occurring.

"We need more light," said Gwyn, adjusting the brightness setting on her tricorder. Their surroundings were immediately more visible.

"Look there!" said Dal, pointing toward markings on the cave's wall.

"Look down!" said Jankom Pog.

Dal and Gwyn were so shocked to hear any voice, let alone one so familiar, that they each dropped their tricorders. "Jankom Pog?"

"Jankom Pog!"

Dal and Gwyn struggled to move the rocks and boulders surrounding their crewmate. When they finally got to within arm's length, they saw that the tech attached to Jankom's extendable multi-mitt was trapped under a large boulder.

"Jankom Pog woke up down here," said the Tellarite. "Jankom Pog tried to punch his way through to the surface, but..."

"But instead of busting through, you brought it down on you?" asked Gwyn.

"Yeah," Jankom admitted. "Jankom Pog didn't think it all the way through."

Gwyn shot Dal a look. "There's a lot of that going around."

It took a while, but after some pushing, pulling, and resting, Dal and Gwyn freed Jankom, and his multi-mitt, from the weight of the boulder. The crewmates took some time to catch their breath, get their bearings, and in Jankom's case, rub his bruised arm. His high-tech mech didn't appear to be any worse for wear. There were no scratches or dings to be seen on the retractable cable or forearm covering, but the parts of his right arm not covered with mech did show signs of black-and-blue bruises rising to the surface of his hairy skin. Just as with Dal and Gwyn, his combadge was not able to reach the *Protostar*. After ensuring Jankom's health, Gwyn tried to decipher the markings they'd seen on the cave wall.

"Is it a language?" asked Dal.

Gwyn touched the symbols. "In a way. It looks more like pictures than letters. But there's so much of it that's missing, it's hard to decipher." Gwyn dragged her finger through one of the lines. "Looks like ash. I guess whoever made this used the residue from the fires that kept them warm to leave a message."

"Jankom Pog has an idea! Just because we can't see it doesn't mean it's not there." Jankom adjusted his tricorder's settings and shone it on the cave wall. Suddenly, what were incomplete dark symbols were now a glowing and comprehensive pictogram of a village.

Dal's eyes widened. "What did you do?"

Jankom was triumphant. "Ash is made from burnt wood, and burnt wood has a different chemical composition than whatever that stone is. So even if we couldn't see it, there might still be some stuck into the rock. Jankom set his tricorder to detect and highlight the differences, and ta-da!"

Gwyn was impressed. "Good job, Jankom. Maybe you do know what you're doing. Sometimes."

Jankom agreed. Then he said, "Hey, what do you mean 'sometimes'?"

CHAPTER EIGHT

*T*he mural showed a group of humanoids looking up to the stars. A giant swirl was painted near the largest star.

Looks like a wormhole, thought Gwyn.

Dal searched the wall for more art. "What's this?" He ran his fingers up a crack in the cave wall. "It's too perfectly straight to be natural."

Gwyn approached to inspect it for herself. She extended her fretwork and ran its tip from the roof to the ground. Ancient dirt and sediment fell away. She could feel a weak but steady flow of air coming from it. "It's a seam. Maybe a door to something?"

Jankom pointed his tricorder at it. "Jankom Pog is picking up lots of things. Looks like ... water? And food! Oh, and lots of energy, too."

The friends' moods immediately lightened. Jankom scanned the surface again to locate an access point. They pushed and pulled on the stone wall until, finally, it budged, opening into what looked like a wartime bunker. It was about the size of the captain's quarters onboard the *Protostar*. But rather than containing a single large bed and ample room for a workstation and dining and seating areas, the space was packed with twenty cots. Pillows and blankets were strewn everywhere. And instead of featuring decorations and artwork, these stone walls were lined with shelves packed with enough stores of food and water to last through a siege.

Gwyn blew some dust off one of the shelves. "It doesn't look like this was ever used."

Dal picked up a can. He couldn't read the label, but based on the sloshing sound he heard, he assumed it contained something drinkable. He popped the top and took a sip.

"Wait!" cried Gwyn. "You don't know what that is!"

"Jankom Pog thinks the food on Tars Lamora was better than this slop," Jankom said, already surrounded by a collection of half-eaten and -drunk provisions.

How can he eat so quickly? Gwyn thought. She accepted a water can from Dal and took a long, welcome drink.

Dal sat on a cot and looked around the abandoned room. "I guess whoever built this bunker never got a chance to use it?"

Gwyn nodded. "Watchers never give anyone a chance to do anything. But why was the bunker built? And how? None of it makes any sense."

Jankom collapsed onto a cot and immediately started snoring.

"Not a bad idea," said Dal, relaxing himself down onto his back.

Gwyn didn't want to admit how tired she was, but resting did seem like a good idea. As her eyes began to close, Gwyn felt the faintest of breezes move her braided hair. Turning her face toward the wall, she could feel a slight airflow coming from behind one of the shelving units. She turned to Dal and Jankom. Both were fast asleep. Gwyn shrugged. It was probably nothing. Just the normal engineered airflow in one of these kinds of holds. If people were going to be hiding for a while, they needed to make sure they had access to clean, fresh air. The chemicals found in the stagnant air beneath the surface of any planet were potentially deadly.

Gwyn tried to rest, but her curiosity was getting the better of her, and she needed to see how the exhaust system was configured. She followed the breeze to a section on the shelf empty of any cans, bottles, or boxes. There, beside a bent metal grate, was a frame. Its metal edges faced sharply inward. Gwyn aimed her tricorder at the bent frame. Scorch marks. Old but not ancient. Something came through that vent into the room. She pointed her tricorder toward the shelf and around the frame. Organic. Liquid. Blood.

Gwyn began to put the pieces together. This wasn't a never-used bunker. It was used. By people hiding from the Watchers. But though they'd entered the room through the door, they were taken out through the air vents. Air vents that were just big enough for Watchers to get through. She turned toward her sleeping friends and opened her mouth to yell a warning. But stopped herself before uttering a sound. There was no indication that the Watchers knew where they were, and the chances of them thinking to use the air vent to find them in a bunker that had been empty of life for so long was next to none. So instead of waking her crewmates, she decided to let them sleep. It was the least she could do given how complicit she'd been in exhausting them for so many years on Tars Lamora.

Gwyn took one more look in the vent. Once she was sure she couldn't see any red lights in the darkness, she pulled blankets up over Dal's and Jankom's shoulders. Satisfied that they were warm and deeply asleep, she pulled a cot to the open door and sat, fretwork extended, on its edge. *Let them sleep,* she thought. *I'll stand guard.*

CHAPTER NINE

Dal and Jankom woke to find Gwyn still at her post. Rested, or at least as rested as they thought they could be before the Watchers made it to them, the three friends took a moment to eat and drink a little more, then started off on their way farther into the tunnels.

As they walked, they watched as the markings on the walls became more and more dense. Rather than arbitrarily turning left or right, or even following the directions spat out by their tricorders, they followed the progression of the pictograms through what looked like a village, a town, and then a city. And as the story unfolded, they came to understand that the planet was once home to a growing and thriving society of humanoids. Starting off as hunter-gatherers and farmers, they eventually came together to form collectives for everyone's benefit.

After walking through the murals for about an hour, the pictograms changed in both level of sophistication and medium. The ash that had replaced the scratches was itself replaced by paint and then ink. Gwyn was amazed. "This is incredible. Advanced technology fused into stone!"

"Yeah, incredible stone technology. I was thinking that too, Gwyn," agreed Dal.

Without further need for any sort of spectral or chemical analysis, Jankom turned his tricorder away from the cave walls and in the direction they were going. Soon enough, the paint was replaced with some sort of glowing compound that lit up the cave so much, they could clearly see the walls and tunnels that lay before them. The stories continued. Towns became cities, cities became metropolises. Arts and commerce thrived. Gwyn was happy to see that children were valued, educated, and taught to carry on local traditions of doing good works.

"An intellectual society built this tunnel. So what happened to them?" Gwyn wondered.

Dal grimaced as he looked ahead at the next set of images. "The Watchers are what happened to them."

The once vital and vibrant cities were soon reduced to rubble. Images of crying bipeds were all around them.

Gwyn's shoulders dropped. "They were conquered. Then imprisoned."

They'd come to a dead end of the tunnel as well as the story. Gwyn approached the last image. An object being shot up and away from the planet. She approached the wall and placed her hand on the picture of the object.

"Is that … ?" Dal half asked, knowing the answer.

Gwyn nodded her head. "It's the doll. It was an SOS."

"What's an SOS?" asked Jankom.

"It means help!" Gwyn shouted. "Help that never came. Help that we're too late to give." She pounded the wall in frustration.

"This. Just. Got. Serious." Dal took a step back, right into the wall behind him. Suddenly, the wall that had blocked them from going any farther slid back. "I meant to do that!" he said, falling out of the cave and onto the sand of the planet's surface.

Gwyn walked over to him. "We'd probably been making a smooth and steady incline for a while. Didn't even notice we were headed up."

"Or notice this!" Dal stared at an enormous, dormant machine.

Jankom inspected it from all angles. A series of control panels, crowded with buttons, screens, and levers surrounded a clear tube that extended up to the sky. "Looks like a dead battery."

Gwyn checked her tricorder. "Yeah. There's a trace amount of energy going up from it."

Dal leaned over. "And it looks like it goes all the way down into the planet, too. As deep as we were."

"Maybe," mused Gwyn. "But why?"

Suddenly, Jankom Pog's combadge sprang to life. "Janeway to Jankom. Can you read me?"

"Jankom Pog can! Jankom Pog can!" he shouted. "Three to beam up!"

"Jankom, wait—" cried Gwyn. But before she could finish, she, Jankom, and Dal dematerialized.

CHAPTER TEN

Hologram Janeway rushed to the teleporter pad. "Are you all right? I've been trying to contact you for hours!"

Dal brushed off her concern. "Totally fine, Janeway. I had everything under control."

"And Jankom Pog was totally under a rock!" Jankom said, hopping off the pad and brushing the sand from his hair. "Jankom Pog is going to get some ADB."

Gwyn watched as he sauntered out of the transporter room into the corridor. *Unbelievable,* she thought. *Both of them.*

"Dal," Janeway continued, "what happened down there?"

Gwyn sat on the steps leading down from the

pad. She was hungry and tired. It didn't matter that she was uncomfortable. None of that seemed to really matter now. "What happened is that we were too late. They're all gone. The Watchers got them all."

Janeway was shocked. "The Watchers?"

Dal answered this time. "It's true, Janeway. Looks like it happened a while ago. There wasn't anyone around, but there were Watchers. Hundreds of them. Probably thousands."

"Fascinating. That explains those unexplainable energy signatures Zero reported. At least some of them. How did they get there? Why?"

Gwyn realized everyone was waiting for her to answer. She shrugged.

Janeway didn't want to put any more pressure on the crew, so she moved on. "Well, all of that will have to wait. We have a much more pressing concern at the moment. I'll meet you on the bridge."

Janeway disappeared, leaving Dal and Gwyn alone in the transporter room.

Dal extended his hand to Gwyn. "Are you okay?"

"No," she replied, letting him help her up. "And I have a feeling that things are going to get worse."

"Things are going to get so much worse!" shouted Jankom Pog as Gwyn and Dal arrived on the *Protostar*'s bridge. "Tell them about it with ac-ro-nyms, Janeway. We don't have time for full words!"

Janeway waited for Dal and Gwyn to approach the console she and Jankom Pog were looking at. "In this case, I think it's more important to be clear than quick, Jankom."

"What's going on?" Dal asked.

Janeway fixed her gaze on a display showing a collection of scientific readings. "Our scans seem to indicate that the Dyson sphere that's enveloping the sunstar is failing. At an alarming rate. Fissure eruptions are causing shock waves and extraordinary energy surges."

"Was that what hit the ship earlier?" asked Dal.

"No doubt about it. We were caught in the blast emanating from right here." Janeway pointed at the screen. The crew watched the computer simulation of how a massive blast of energy erupted from the Dyson sphere and hit the *Protostar* and the three orbiting planets. "We did sustain some damage from the shock wave. Nothing that can't be fixed manually, though. Aside from the few seconds it took to beam you three back onboard, I've kept our shields raised to minimize any further damage."

Dal nodded his head. "Could the blast have affected our combadges, too?"

"Absolutely. It was strong and bright enough to push some of the ship's sensors and comms offline, so it makes sense to think it could do the same to your personal devices." She opened her holographic hand to reveal two new combadges. "Once I realized I couldn't hail you, I assumed that to be the case. I took the liberty of replicating new ones for you."

Gwyn and Dal accepted the new hardware. They affixed the iconic Starfleet symbol, reminiscent of an arrowhead, to their uniforms.

Jankom Pog wants a new one too, the engineer thought. *Just because Jankom's combadge started working again doesn't mean it's not all scratched up.*

Dal was grateful for Janeway's ingenuity. "Thanks, Janeway. You really saved us all!"

"Not all, Dal," Janeway said, lowering her chin. "Not yet."

Dal suddenly realized that Rok-Tahk, Zero, and Murf were not there. How could he not have noticed that the second he stepped onto the bridge? "Where . . ."

"Even though we couldn't communicate, your combadges emitted a strong enough signal for me to easily pinpoint where you three were on the first planet." She brushed that planet off the display. "Unfortunately, I'm unable to get many readings from the second or third planets. There are enormous amounts of covalent energy mooring the Dyson sphere to those planets. And though there's no active connection between the sunstar and the planet you were just on, the *Protostar* is showing a trace amount of energy, so we can only assume that all three planets were, at one time, tied to their sunstar."

"That explains the dead battery we found," said Dal.

Gwyn hoped that whoever built the machine, whoever the Watchers *forced* to build the machine, were successful in shutting it down before they were eradicated.

"Maybe. But even without a third active connection, there's enough energy coming off just those two tethers to keep our sensors from registering much of anything. But I've been scanning each planet for life-forms sector by sector. It's a slow process, but accurate." With a squeeze of her fingers, the image zoomed in onto two small pulsing dots, indicating two individual forms of life on the second planet. "And I found two life signs here."

Gwyn squinted at the display. "But that's only two. Where's the other?"

Janeway took a deep holographic breath. "I don't know."

Gwyn tried not to gasp. Janeway straightened her holographic back confidently. "I don't know ... yet. As I said, it's taking longer than I'd like, but Starfleet never gives up. We just need patience."

Dal's mind raced. "How much time do we have, Janeway?"

"Not much," she said, once again refocusing the stellar map onto the Dyson sphere. "The explosions emanating from the fissures are increasing in frequency, duration, and intensity. Most have been occurring planet-side or at least far enough away from us to not cause too much trouble. I've been able to maneuver the *Protostar* to avoid the ones that have headed our way, and the shields are helping and holding. But everything indicates that we probably don't have much time until the entire sunstar goes supernova."

"Meaning what?" asked Dal, trying to remember even a bit of the astrophysics he'd been studying.

"Meaning," said Janeway solemnly, "that the sunstar will explode. And if it does—when it does—everything in this system, including those three planets and, if we're not out of here, us, will be destroyed. Oh, I should mention one more thing," said Janeway.

"One more thing? How much more could there be?" asked Dal.

"Our sensors are also showing an emerging wormhole near the sunstar. It may or may not be related to anything, but at the rate it's growing, it looks like it will reach full size around the same time as the sunstar goes supernova."

"Is that it? Are there any more things?" Dal asked.

"Not that I know of. Yet."

Gwyn sat on the armrest of Dal's captain's seat. "How much time, exactly, is 'not much' time?"

Janeway ran a quick calculation and confirmed her results with several of the *Protostar*'s systems. "Forty hours, give or take."

"Give or take?" asked Dal.

"Well, all time is relative, but in this case ..."

"We need to get out of here," said Jankom.

"We need to find our friends!" countered Gwyn.

They looked at Dal to be the tiebreaker. To make a decision. To be the captain.

"Okay," Dal said, "here's the plan."

CHAPTER ELEVEN

Jankom walked with Dal and Gwyn along one of the *Protostar*'s corridors until they arrived at an intersection. "So just to make sure Jankom Pog understands. Jankom Pog is going to stay here on the *Protostar* with Janeway. Jankom Pog will fix the damage while Janeway searches for the third life sign."

"Right," said Dal.

"And you two are going to beam down to the planet."

"Right."

"The planet we know nothing about."

"Right."

"To see whether the two life signs Janeway found are two of our missing friends. And if it is them, you will get them back here."

"Right."

"And if it's not them?"

"We'll see if we can help."

"And if that planet's filled with Watchers too?"

Dal threw his shoulders back. "I've got a plan!"

"Okay. Jankom Pog understands." The engineer flexed his multi-mitt and turned left down the corridor on his way to make repairs. "Jankom Pog is glad he's the one staying on the ship."

Gwyn and Dal turned right toward the transporter room.

Gwyn positioned herself on one of the teleporter pads. "What is the plan, Dal?"

"Eh, we'll figure it out. Janeway, energize!"

"We can't just—" Once again, Gwyn was interrupted by an unexpected dematerialization.

"—figure it out, Dal," Gwyn continued as they rematerialized on the planet's surface. "And if you think—"

Gwyn interrupted herself this time. She looked around and marveled at the enormous and well-lit room they found themselves in. Each and every square inch of the walls, from the floor to the impossibly high ceiling, was stacked with neatly rolled scrolls. Tables and desks were placed throughout the hall.

Dal's combadge sprang to life. *"Janeway to away team."*

"We've arrived safely, Janeway."

"Acknowledged. But where are you?"

"I'm in heaven," said Gwyn, smiling for what seemed to be the first time since finding the doll on Odaru.

Janeway was confused. *"Where?"*

"We're not in heaven, Janeway," Dal corrected. "It's only a library."

"A library?" Janeway's voice bounced. *"I am fan girling with Gwyn. I love libraries!"*

Dal liked libraries too, but Gwyn seemed to be in another dimension. "Gwyn, if you can focus for a minute, maybe something in here is useful?"

Gwyn walked over to one of the desks. A large open scroll and an overturned chair lay beside it. "Everything in a library is useful, Dal," she said. "But this may be especially useful. It's like someone was reading this and left in a hurry."

Gwyn scanned the hand-drawn symbols filling the scroll with her tricorder. "Sending you the text from one of these scrolls now, Janeway."

"*Received. Running it through the universal translator. This may take a few minutes.*"

Dal righted the chair and took a seat. It was much less comfortable than his captain's chair. "Remember how your father banned universal translators on Tars?"

Gwyn nodded. "He always said, 'Prisoners who cannot communicate cannot rebel.'"

"How'd that work out for him?"

Before Gwyn could answer, Janeway's voice came through. "*Interesting. According to the translation, it seems the inhabitants of this planet called themselves Naroans. It says that this planet is called Mirios. You were just on Orisi, and the other planet in this system is called Taresse.*"

Gwyn, still amazed to be in a library, said, "Imagine how much more knowledge is stored here."

Dal was, for once, more practical in his query. "They can build a giant space generator around a sunstar, but all their stuff was written on scrolls and painted on walls?"

Janeway paused. "*Perhaps there is something to be said for the simpler way of life, even if the Naroans did have access to advanced technology."*

"Weird, but okay," said Dal. "What else can you tell us?"

"Nothing more until you unroll and scan more of the scroll, I'm afraid."

With that, Gwyn approached the scroll and unfurled it slowly, being careful not to rip or damage it. Gwyn jumped back and screamed. Her fretwork reflexively extended from her arm and pierced the scroll right through the table. Dal didn't know whether to rush to help Gwyn or to the table's edge to keep the scroll from spooling off it.

"What is it?" asked Janeway. *"What's going on down there?"*

Gwyn waved her hand, shooing Dal away from her. "We're doomed. That's not my father leading the Watchers."

Dal slowly approached the scroll, the part still fretworked to the table. "That's Drednok!"

CHAPTER TWELVE

Dal searched the scroll for more information. "That's it, Janeway. There's nothing written or left to translate after the drawings of Drednok in pieces, and then being put together."

Gwyn still couldn't believe it. "And then he repaid these inhabitants by destroying their system. Why?"

Janeway acknowledged Dal's transmission. "*Gwyn, did the Diviner have more than one Drednok Lieutenant on Tars Lamora?*"

"No," Gwyn replied to the voice coming from the combadge. "His was the only one. And that one bloodthirsty monster was one too many."

Dal leaned in toward the scroll for a better look. "This must be a different Drednok."

Gwyn nodded. "And it looks like he conquered the

Naroans. All on his own." *This had to have something to do with Solum,* she thought. *How could it not?* Her father, the Diviner, was a clever man. Maybe this was all part of his master plan? To get her to this planet too? Was she a part of this tragedy?

Dal leaned in toward the scroll for a better look. "I'm no art expert, but this doesn't look exactly like your Drednok."

Gwyn flinched at being assigned sole ownership of that monster. Dal quickly realized how he'd accidentally hurt his friend. "*The* Drednok. Ummm... Drednok. Just Drednok. I mean, look at him. This one seems ... meaner than the other one?"

Gwyn squinted her icy-blue eyes for a better look. "He *does* look meaner. I didn't think that was possible, but he definitely looks meaner."

Dal was eager to seize on an opportunity to heal the wound he'd caused. "Totally. He's mean with a weird head. He's just a big ol' Meany Head. Yep, that's not Drednok. That's Meany Head."

Gwyn smirked. "Meany Head." Dal placed a comforting hand on Gwyn's upper arm.

The friends stood in silence until Janeway's voice cut in. "*I hate to interrupt, but I must remind you that* the clock is still ticking. *You have crewmates to find before the sunstar goes supernova.*"

"Right," said Dal, resuming his role as captain. "Where do we go, Janeway?"

"*The coordinates of the two life signs have not changed since I first detected them. We can only hope that they'll remain there until you reach them. Sending those coordinates to your tricorders now. But be careful.*"

Dal checked his tech to confirm the signal was received. "Okay," he said to Gwyn, "let's go."

Dal kept his head down, alternating between looking at his tricorder's directions and where his feet were falling. Gwyn, on the other hand, kept her head up and fretwork out, just in case they came face-to-face with more Watchers or, worse, Meany Head. But instead of danger, she found herself in constant awe of the library's architecture and contents. They passed through countless halls and corridors, each containing countless scrolls and artwork. Whoever the Naroans were, whatever happened to them, they were clearly a people who valued education and history. It stung Gwyn to think that she may have played an unwitting part in their destruction.

Dal stopped before an enormous set of doors. They'd come to the end of this part of their journey. The crewmates nodded to each other and opened the doors.

Before them lay an abandoned city. Though the soaring and artful architecture of Mirios stood in stark contrast to the barren landscapes of Orisi, it presented more, not less, danger to the *Protostar*'s crew. Watchers could be hiding anywhere. The crowded cityscape provided them with an incalculable number of places to hide and to ambush anyone passing through. And if Meany Head was here to lead them, they could launch a calculated and coordinated attack at any moment. Dal and Gwyn knew they had to be even more cautious and watchful of their surroundings. They could hear nothing but the wind blowing through the abandoned buildings and streets.

"Janeway to Dal."

Dal tapped his combadge to acknowledge. "Dal here."

"Just checking in, Captain."

"We're . . . fine? Still walking. How are things up there?"

"*Moving along. Jankom has been repairing the damage. I think he's dawdling a little with the food replicators, though. I'm getting reports of unusually high numbers of sweet radish pies being ordered.*"

"That sounds like Jankom. Well, he's been working hard all day. I guess he could use a break." Dal looked at Gwyn. "We all could."

"*Take care of yourselves,*" Janeway continued. "*Make sure to stop for rest and for something to eat. But not for too long. We've got less than forty hours until the sunstar goes supernova, and you have at least another couple hours of walking before you reach the location of the two life signs. I'm still working on getting our sensors fully back online but will continue the regional scans for additional life signs. Janeway out.*"

"We should listen to the lady," said Dal, taking a seat on the bottom step of a staircase leading up to a building. Gwyn sat on the step above. "You know, I'm not telekinetic or telepathic or any other tele-something, but I can tell when something's wrong. This isn't your fault."

Gwyn turned to him. "You can't know that."

"Neither can you. How could you have done any of this? You were on Tars Lamora with me, remember?"

"I remember all right. It's all I remember."

"So?"

Gwyn stood and started to pace. "So sure, I was there on Tars with you. But if there were two Drednoks, maybe there were two mes? There's so much I don't know. So much my father lied to me about. Hid from me. I can't really know anything for sure."

"You can know some things for sure."

Gwyn turned and stared at Dal. "Like what? What could I know for sure?"

"That I'm your friend," Dal offered.

Gwyn's face softened. "I—" She froze. "Do you hear that?"

Dal cocked his head to one side. Sure enough, the telltale mechanical clicking of Watchers started echoing through the cavernous, empty streets. It was too diffused to know where it was coming from, but it was surely coming. "We gotta go."

Dal and Gwyn ran as fast as they could.

"*Janeway to Dal. Your tricorders are registering elevated levels of adrenaline and a significant rise in heart rate. Is everything okay?*"

"Not now! We've got Watchers on our tail."

"I'm not picking up any energy signatures from your immediate area. Are you sure?"

Dal and Gwyn stopped dead in their tracks.

"You're not?"

A familiar, gruff voice took over the comm. *"Oh, did Janeway forget to mention that Jankom Pog got the* Protostar's *sensors back to ninety percent? Because Jankom Pog did."*

"He did," agreed Janeway. *"Once he finished eating, that is. The energy signatures that match the ones the Watchers emitted on Orisi are still a far distance away from you. In fact, they seem to be congregated in the direct vicinity of the two other energy signatures."*

"Which means?" asked Dal.

Gwyn remembered how the mindlessly and heartlessly programmed Watchers would function as either protectors or jailers on Tars Lamora. "Which means they're either defending those two life signs or jailing them there."

Back on the *Protostar*, Jankom looked to Janeway for guidance. She nodded. *"I'm sending the Watchers' energy signature to your tricorders."*

Dal checked the readout. "So all this time we

thought we were running from the Watchers when..."

"We were actually running toward them." Gwyn sighed as she looked at her own tricorder. "We were just so nervous to hear them that we imagined we did. Just like we knew they were around any and every corner on Tars."

"Well, *I* knew they were around any corner on Tars, at least." Dal was quick to correct her. Too quick to stop himself from inflicting another injury on his friend. He knew nothing that happened on Tars was her fault, but there was a part of him—the scared, traumatized, still-hurting part—that needed to remember that Gwyn was a witness to the Diviner's cruelty.

"That's not fair," she said. Even though, deep down, she believed it to be true.

"I...I know. I'm sorry. I wasn't thinking."

Gwyn turned and started walking. "You never think."

Dal silently agreed.

"Janeway to Dal."

"What's up, Janeway?"

"Just checking in on your progress. It's been a

few hours since you checked in."

"All's ... fine?" Dal looked to Gwyn to either agree or disagree, but she kept staring straight ahead. They'd walked in silence since their fight. Though they were able to rationalize not speaking to each other as an effort to keep audible tabs on any Watchers who left their post, the truth was that each was lost in his or her own memories and trying to think of ways to apologize to the other for things that had happened in the far and immediate past. It wasn't easy. None of this was easy.

"Good. You should be coming up on your destina-tion shortly. Be careful. Report back when you can. Janeway out."

Dal's combadge went silent. As they approached, the Watchers' chattering and chirping was loud and immediate. Now was the time for the crewmates to start taking calculated measures to avoid being detected by the Watchers' sensors or visual scans. Hiding behind statues, vehicles, and the other physical remnants of a now-defunct but-once-thriving society, they slowly approached their destination.

Dal and Gwyn peeked around a corner to see

a battalion of Watchers scurrying in front of a building. The building was heavily fortified with walls too thick for their tricorders to penetrate, so they were forced to visually assess their situation. The building towered six stories aboveground, and who knew how many below. Pieces of demolished Watchers littered both sides of the spiked gate that surrounded it. Gwyn wondered if there had been a skirmish or two here, and if so, who had been fighting the Watchers. So far, the Watchers seemed to have retained control of the building.

Until now, Gwyn thought. *I hope.*

"I know you well enough to know you don't have a plan," Gwyn whispered to her crewmate.

Dal looked offended. "Well, as it so happens, I do have a plan."

"Oh?"

"Yep. We get past the Watchers, enter the building, rescue whoever's in there, find out what's going on, then get back to the *Protostar*, out of this star system, and on to Starfleet."

"That's the plan?"

"That's the plan!"

"That's not a plan. That's a to-do list."

Oh, it's most definitely a plan, thought Dal.

"And how do you *plan* on executing this plan?" asked Gwyn.

"Please don't use the word 'execute,'" stammered Dal, suddenly distracted by the thought of winding up on one of the gate's spikes. *That's it!* he realized. "We need a distraction."

Dal's mind raced with possibilities. Or the lack thereof. "I got it!" he said. "Come with me."

Gwyn reluctantly followed Dal as they approached the gate.

"You know we're heading toward danger now, right?" she asked.

"Don't be such a sourpuss," he said.

Gwyn was a master at translation and communication, but even experts couldn't know everything. "What's a 'sourpuss'?" she asked.

"You, that's what. But you can't be a sourpuss if you follow my directions."

Gwyn was skeptical, but she didn't want to be a sourpuss, whatever that was, so she reluctantly listened to what Dal had to say.

Keeping low to the ground, Gwyn crept slowly closer and closer to the gate, until she was in a fretwork's length of a downed Watcher. Activating her neuroflux, she mentally extended the metal as far as she could, hooking it onto the Watcher's carcass and dragging it toward her.

Once the carcass was in hand, she held it to her body as she'd once held the Odarunian doll, and retreated to where Dal waited for her.

"Now what?" she asked, handing him the deactivated killing machine.

"*Now Jankom Pog takes over!*"

"Shhhh!" They shushed the too-loud voice coming from Dal's combadge.

"*Sorry. Jankom Pog got too excited.*"

Dal carefully followed Jankom's instructions on how to reactivate and control the Watcher's systems.

This would be a lot easier with a visual, he thought, *or even if Jankom was here to do it himself. Scratch that, it's probably best he's not.*

Jankom had gained lots of firsthand knowledge of the Watchers' operating system while on Tars. He was often lucky enough to scavenge some of their spare parts for side projects, or to repair outdated and damaged mining equipment. But this was a first. He'd never reanimated one remotely before. It was oddly exciting.

He instructed Dal on how to find the Watcher's main battery and how to power it up by connecting it to Dal's combadge. The Watcher's red eye started to glow. Its legs slowly worked through the rust and dust clogging its gears. Dal and Gwyn looked at each other, hoping this would work. Dal set the deadly machine down on the ground, took a step back, and held his tricorder. He tapped a button, and the Watcher suddenly jumped and turned toward them, and waited for instructions. It worked! The tricorder, linked to Dal's combadge, now acted as a remote control. Dal tested the connectivity by instructing the machine to go left, then right, then charge up its stinger tail.

"Well done, Jankom!" Gwyn said.

Her combadge came to life. *"Jankom Pog is a good engineer!"*

Dal looked around for his own bit of praise. "I helped too!"

Janeway's voice came through loud and clear. *"You're down to only one combadge, so you'll have to stick together."*

"Understood," said Gwyn, "but before we worry about separating, we have to worry about getting into the citadel."

"On it," said Dal.

The remote-controlled Watcher, now at Dal's command, turned toward his former compatriots.

"Don't go too fast," warned Gwyn. "This has to be a surprise attack."

Dal scrunched his face in disbelief. "Can you give me some credit? I know what I'm doing."

The remote-controlled Watcher started walking at a casual pace—or at least as casual a pace as a mechanical killing machine could walk. Gwyn relaxed just enough to then see the Watcher suddenly sprint into a group of three others. Hopping onto one and impaling it with its stinger tail, it spun quickly to grab and throw the second into the third Watcher, hurling them both offline and into a nearby wall. It hopped into the still sizzling duo and quickly ripped off two of their legs, using them as bayonets to stab, slash, and otherwise incapacitate the other Watchers it was taking by surprise.

In less time than Gwyn could process what was happening and tell Dal to stop, the entirety of the mechanical legion guarding the citadel had been demolished.

"And that," said Dal, leaning against a wall casually, "is how that's done."

Dal reported back to the *Protostar*, making sure Janeway understood that his triumph was officially recorded into the ship's log as DVW Day (short for Dal's Victory over the Watchers Day).

"I'm proud of you, but let's hold off on assigning any honorifics until you and the rest of the crew are back safely onboard, Captain," responded Janeway.

Dal wasn't quite ready to release his Watcher from his control yet, so he kept it on a virtual leash, letting it walk fifty paces in front of them, as he and Gwyn entered the building.

Gwyn noticed Dal smirking just a bit. "Oh, how the tables have burned, huh?"

"What?"

"You being in control of a Watcher instead of the other way around?"

"Oh—you mean tables. How the tables have *turned.*"

"Isn't that what I said?"

"No, you said . . ."

"HELP!"

"That's Rok's voice!" cried Gwyn.

Gwyn and Dal ran so fast, they overtook their pet Watcher.

"We're coming! We're coming!" they shouted down the abandoned corridors until they came to a giant metallic door.

Pushing with all their might, they found an enormous generator, a twin of the dead one they'd found on Orisi. But this one was very much alive and throbbing with incalculable energy. Dal wiped the sweat from his forehead. Light, brighter than the *Protostar*'s warp drive, was contained within some sort of clear solid barrier that directed it up and out of the power station into the sky above them.

"Dal! Gwyn!" Rok shouted. "My heroes!"

"Friends," said Zero, who was stuck with Rok-Tahk in a cell too small for either of them to move. "It is a pleasure to lay my eye on you again. I almost lost hope."

Dal approached his crewmates. "As a wise Medusan once said: 'While others give up hope, I cling to it!'"

"Hey! I am a wise Medusan! You are quoting me!"

"You bet I am!"

Gwyn knelt just outside the glowing energy field and tested its strength with her fretwork. Sparks flew. "We have to shut the power down, Dal."

"On it," he said, searching the walls for an off switch.

"What happened, Rok?" asked Gwyn, not moving from her spot. She knew how scared her young friend must have been.

"The transporter beamed me into this power station. At first it was cool—cuz, you know, it's SCIENCE! But then the Watchers locked me in."

Gwyn tried to comfort her. "We'll get you out of here, don't worry. What about you, Z?"

"After the transporter malfunction, I landed here—a fascinating planet—but a Watcher patrol disrupted my investigations. It was quite rude of them, really."

"A Watcher!" screamed Rok, pointing to the idling remote-controlled mech. Unable to move more than just an inch, she pressed herself as far into the back wall as she could—pushing Zero ever so slightly toward the force field. Their metallic outer casing sizzled on contact with the energy.

"Don't worry, Rok," said Dal, "this Watcher is working for us."

Rok-Tahk relaxed just enough for Zero to back away. They would have raised an eyebrow in disbelief had they had one. "A Watcher working for us? That's a novel concept."

Dal searched for a way to power down the energy field for the better part of an hour. He ventured out into the rest of the power station, the pet Watcher leading the way, but couldn't find any other room that looked like a control center. He returned and searched for a button or lever to try on the console surrounding the generator. Lights flashed and screens provided readouts of energy fluctuations and readings that Dal couldn't understand. Hitting the wrong button or engaging the wrong sequence could be disastrous. He didn't want to accidentally kill his crew by initiating a power surge or a self-destruct sequence instead of saving them by powering it down.

Dal looked up and watched as the green and yellow energy dissipated into an invisible version of itself and connected, somehow, some way, high up above them, to the Dyson sphere.

Gwyn used the time to fill in Rok-Tahk and Zero on what had happened on the first planet and back on the *Protostar*. *This must be what it's like*, she thought, *in another life, to tell a bedtime story*. Hidden tunnels, unstoppable enemies stopped by Gwyn, Dal, and Jankom using their smarts and a little bit of luck, a giant citadel, and a daring rescue. All they needed now was a happy ending. *Please let us have a happy ending*. Once Zero and Rok were fully up to date, Gwyn turned to Dal. "Anything? Time's ticking."

"I know, I know. Nothing."

Rok-Tahk had been watching Dal and his remote-controlled Watcher as intently as she'd been listening to Gwyn.

"Those Watchers sure are strong," she said. "What if instead of using it to hurt the other Watchers, you try using it to hurt the generator?"

"What do you mean?" asked Dal.

"Well, if its casing is strong enough to go through another Watcher, it's probably strong enough to go through the control panel and into the chamber to disrupt the matter-antimatter assembly," Rok theorized. "And if this machine is anything like the *Protostar*'s warp core, even if we can't shut it down completely, we might at least be able to shove it offline long enough for us to roll out of here."

Dal was, as usual, impressed by his young crewmate's engineering expertise. Once again, her brains were going to save them all.

"Let's try it!" Dal directed the Watcher to hop onto the generator's console. "Thanks for your help," he whispered, before ordering it to use its insectlike legs and tail to ravage into the control panel.

The crewmates held their breath until, after a few moments, the lights from the generator and the force field began to flicker, and then they all went dark. Dal sighed in great relief as Zero exited the cell, their metal containment suit dented in the spots Rok-Tahk had been leaning on.

Rok tumbled out and stretched to her full height.

"Group hug!" she shouted, embracing Gwyn and Zero.

"Not yet," said Gwyn, pulling away. "No group hugs until we find Murf."

Rok's eyes went wide. "Murf's missing? We gotta find Murf!"

CHAPTER THIRTEEN

Janeway's voice echoed in the room. *"Janeway to away team!"*

"We're here, Janeway!" replied Gwyn.

"Are you safe? Have you found Zero and Rok?"

"I'm here!" shouted Rok-Tahk, waving to the air surrounding Janeway's disembodied voice. "Zero and I were stuck in a cell for a really long time. My neck's all crampy and my butt's asleep and I'm really hungry and I think I stepped on a pebble or something, but it's not so bad except when I—"

"I'm here too," said Zero, trying to pound out their dents.

"And we're all fine," said Gwyn.

"I can hear that!" said Janeway. *"Something has disrupted the energy coupling Mirios to the Dyson*

sphere, so I can scan the entire planet. Your life signs are all reading as good and strong. Your adrenaline levels and respiration are all elevated, but that's to be expected given the circumstances."

"I was able to shut down the generator," said Dal.

Rok placed her hands on her hips. "With help."

"A lot of help," Dal agreed.

"Well, that explains a lot!" said Janeway. "But not everything."

"What else could there be?" asked Gwyn.

Janeway paused for a beat. "It doesn't explain the Naroan life sign I'm reading!"

The *Protostar*'s crew froze in place as Janeway continued. "I'm sending coordinates to you now. It looks like it should take you about an hour to reach them."

Gwyn couldn't believe it. A Naroan? Maybe they weren't too late to help. "How do you know it's Naroan?"

"The transporter filters out all matter, including DNA that isn't yours, when you beam back onto the ship."

"Why?" asked Dal.

"Transporter accidents are infrequent, but common enough. You wouldn't want a duplicate you showing up any more than you would want a you that's merged with another species, would you?"

"Wait, what do you mean they're 'common enough'?" asked Dal.

"*Remind me to tell you about Tuvix sometime,*" said Janeway. "*My point is, the transporter filtered out anything that wasn't you—including some DNA that you must have picked up when handling the supplies in the bunker on Orisi. I cross-referenced it with Starfleet species databases and confirmed that it was, indeed, Naroan.*"

Gwyn stiffened her posture. "How much time have we got until the sunstar goes supernova, Janeway?"

"*Do you really want to know?*"

"Not really."

"*That's what I thought. You do have some time to rest, though. You've been through a lot, and no Starfleet crew can work efficiently without a little self-care. I'll beam down some provisions to your location now.*"

A shipping container materialized in the room. Rok opened it and found rations of water and food, and one very big, very fluffy pillow. "This for my butt?" she asked.

"It is!" replied Janeway.

"Thanks, Janeway."

Gwyn waited for Dal to tell them it was time to get going. And waited. Finally, after all the food was eaten and Rok could feel her butt again, Gwyn took it upon herself to get them moving.

"Time to get moving. Right, Dal?"

"Right!" he said. "Let's boldly go find that Naroan!"

Janeway's coordinates led them straight to what looked like a storm-cellar door.

Dal pushed on the door. It didn't budge.

Dal pushed again. Still nothing. "Hello? Anyone in there? Please be nice, please be nice."

"Ugh!" cried Gwyn. "These are the right coordinates, but the place is deserted."

"I sense a consciousness behind the door," said Zero.

"Or," Dal suggested, "it's the perfect place for an ambush."

But Zero could sense the life-form beyond the door. "Whoever it is, is afraid. Very afraid."

"Keep going," said Janeway over the open

channel, *"but please proceed with caution."*

Dal knew time was of the essence. "We don't have time for this! Rok, do your thing."

"My thing? What's my thing?" the young Brikar asked.

"Get us in there!"

"Ummmm...okay. Stand aside, friends. Consider this a thank-you for saving my Brikar butt!" Rok-Tahk bent down and pushed on the handles as Dal had. Nothing. Then she gently pulled and the door opened smoothly. "I did my thing!"

Dal almost wished he would fall into another hole and this time stay there forever. "I must have loosened it for her." Gwyn gave him a look.

They walked down the steep stairs to a bunker that resembled the one they'd been in on Orisi. But this one was much bigger. Dim light illuminated the space enough for them to see hundreds of cots and workspaces surrounded by roughly hewn walls lined with shelves and shelves of provisions. Zero motioned to their crewmates to remain silent and follow them toward the consciousness they could sense hiding behind a workstation.

Gwyn didn't need the Medusan's telepathic

abilities to know the Naroan was there, though. She could see, on a table piled with scrap metal and parts, a still-glowing laser welder. It was obvious that whoever was working there was still there.

Silently and slowly, the team separated and approached the workstation from different sides. Gwyn and Zero to the left, Rok-Tahk and Dal to the right. They all looked to Dal for the signal to move, and he raised his hand and, using his fingers, counted down: 3—2—

Suddenly, a figure jumped out from behind the workstation. Almost as tall as Rok, with white hair and beard framing its fishlike face, the creature aimed something right at them.

"Stand back!" it yelled through its pouty lips. "I won't hesitate to use this!" The device seemed small in the creature's long pink fingers, but Gwyn knew just because something was small didn't mean it wasn't deadly.

Gwyn extended her fretwork defensively.

Rok was suddenly giddy. "Ooooh—I've never seen one of these in person!" She grabbed the square handheld device and poked at the two metallic rods protruding from it.

"What is it?" asked Zero.

"It's a self-sealing stem bolt!"

"What does it do?"

"Yes," said the creature, raising a white eyebrow above its downturned, sad-looking eyes. "What *does* it do?"

Rok-Tahk held it up to take a good look. "It, ummm... self-seals?"

Gwyn's patience had run out. "Sorry to interrupt this engineering lesson, but who are you?"

"Who am I? Who are you?" asked the Naroan.

"We're the crew of the Federation starship *Protostar*. I'm Captain Dal R'El."

The creature's long droopy ears perked up. "Federation? Starfleet?! Oh, thank goodness! I'm saved! Starfleet got my message! Oh, we're all saved! Starfleet is here to save us!"

"Saved from what? Who's saved? Who are you?" asked Dal.

"Apologies. Many ages have passed since I saw another living creature. Peace be with you. My name is Yarm'orn, Captain. And you have saved me and saved all Naroans from Star Killer."

CHAPTER FOURTEEN

Jankom Pog beamed down to his crewmates' location. He was interested in exploring some of the spare parts and other tech found in Yarm'orn's workshop. While he rummaged through boxes of reusable and upcyclable stuff, Dal opened a channel back to the *Protostar* so Janeway could hear and record everything Yarm'orn was saying.

"Many centuries ago, we Naroans came here looking for a new home. It was treacherous and few of us made it. Each of the three planets in this system had its own unique and harsh climate. We learned that in order for any one planet to survive, we must all work together to ensure that they all survive. So we existed in a symbiotic peace that benefited the entire system. The hot deserts of Orisi, the frigid, snowy Taresse, and the drowned plains of Mirios all shared technology that made each planet livable. Orisi drew on Taresse's colder temperatures and Mirios's humidity; Taresse benefited from Orisi's warmth and the minerals from Mirios's fertile soil; and we here on Mirios made use of Orisi's aridity and Taresse's winds. Linked by on-planet facilities powered by our sunstar, the climates of all three planets were regulated, but perhaps more than that, the residents of all three planets were united. But everything changed when Star Killer arrived."

While Jankom Pog half listened, Dal, Gwyn, Rok-Tahk, and Zero anxiously waited for Yarm'orn to continue his story. He absentmindedly twirled his long, braided white beard. "Some time ago we found the creature we now call Star Killer—damaged, like it had fallen from the sky." Yarm'orn took a sharp breath, as if the memory hurt him as much physically as it did emotionally. "We repaired it, and when its systems came online, it turned on us. It was cruel beyond measure. It constructed an army of machines that enslaved us. We were forced to build the creature a device that would enlarge the wormhole near our sunstar. We never understood why. We still don't, but we think it has something to do with him wanting to travel through time."

"Drednok, I mean Star Killer, came from the past?" Gwyn asked.

"No. The future."

Dal looked at Gwyn. "Just like your father, Gwyn."

Yarm'orn continued. "The machines took our families. The creature threatened to kill them. What choice did we have but to do what it told us? We were a peaceful race. We had no defenses to speak of. What would we have to defend ourselves against?" Zero placed their mechanical hand on Yarm'orn's. They could psychically sense how much emotional pain the Naroan was in.

"We didn't know how to defend ourselves, so we quickly fell under his control. Star Killer enslaved us all. He even blocked all communication between the planets. We were effectively cut off from one another. Unable to communicate."

The *Protostar* crew knew this tactic from their time on Tars Lamora. If you stop communication between the oppressed, it is harder for them to rise up and rebel. This Star Killer may not be Drednok, but he certainly acted like him.

"Most of us were forced to destroy the hundreds of outposts that kept our planets in symbiosis. All but three were torn to the ground. One on each planet. Our scientists and engineers were tortured until they reconfigured those facilities to become generators that drew from each planet's core, linking them together, and to the sunstar, to create a Dyson sphere to power up the wormhole device. The climates of each planet began to change. Slowly at first, but before too long it became clear that each planet was reverting to its original and deadly state. Orisi became a desolate and deserted wasteland. The temperature on Taresse began to fall. And here on Mirios, well, it's just a matter of time before the oceans rise again and we're all underwater."

"And the sunstar?" asked Gwyn.

"The sunstar. We began to detect signs of trouble early on. Our scientists—each and every one an expert—showed Star Killer data that proved the Dyson sphere was unstable and would lead to the sunstar going supernova. They couldn't predict when it would happen, but they knew it would happen. Eventually. But nothing we said or did could convince Star Killer to stop building it. We never understood why he was doing this. Why he was so willing to destroy our planets and our people. It was impossible to reason with him."

Rok's eyes began to well with tears. She understood what it was like to feel helpless and hopeless. "What did you do?"

"Some of us fought back. And paid the price. Star Killer's robots are harsh taskmasters."

A voice came from the corner of the room. "Jankom Pog knows what you went through." He'd been listening more intently than anyone had thought.

"Some of us tried to escape. But our starships were never designed for fast or long-distance travel. We only ever needed to travel between our three planets. Some of us went into hiding. We'd spend the days working nonstop digging tunnels and mining under Star Killer's orders, and at night, rather than sleep, we built secret bunkers underground to take refuge in. We didn't know what would get us first—our collapsing climates, Star Killer, or our sunstar going supernova. And some of us tried to send for help. I was one of them. I used whatever I could find."

Yarm'orn waved his hand toward the bits and pieces of metal and wire on his workstation.

Jankom Pog held up the doll he'd beamed down with. "Like this?"

Yarm'orn's wide mouth grew into a bright smile. "Yes! Star Killer's security was a little lax at the beginning of his occupation. We were able to sneak two small starships off Mirios. We said they were headed to Orisi for supplies, but we altered their navigation signatures and hoped Star Killer wouldn't realize they were really headed to Odaru until it was too late to stop them. We knew he'd destroyed one of the ships shortly after realizing our deception. But we never knew about the second. The one carrying the children. I gave that to a young boy. He could never have traveled with a data card or isolinear chip—those are too small and easy to lose. But a doll? A doll would be held close and kept safe by any child."

Children, thought Gwyn. *There* were *children*. "We found it in a marketplace on Odaru."

Yarm'orn wrapped his long arms around himself and rocked slowly. "So they did make it to Odaru. They escaped. They survived."

Gwyn took the doll from Jankom and gave it to Yarm'orn. "Yes. They made it."

CHAPTER FIFTEEN

Zero thought it was only fair to tell Yarm'orn everything that had happened since they had arrived: from the shock wave to transporting down to the planets, to fighting the Watchers, to shutting down the generator, to now.

"Where is everyone else?" asked Zero.

Yarm'orn looked at the doll like an old friend. "They're hidden in the underground tunnels on Taresse. I'm the only one on Mirios and the only Naroan who comes to the surface anymore. I can't help myself from trying to find ways to send for help. But now that you're here, my work is done and we'll all be saved!"

Dal stepped toward Yarm'orn. "Hold up, Yarmie. We'd love to help. But our priority is finding our friend, and once we find him, we are outta here."

Gwyn shot Dal a look of disbelief. "You've seen what the Watchers do, what Meany ... Star Killer has done. How could we just leave?"

"How could we not?" Dal countered. "Murf's missing, and the sunstar's about to go supernova in . . . Janeway, how much longer before the whole thing goes *kaboom, splat, blam*?"

"Four hours and thirty minutes, Dal."

"Hear that? Four hours and thirty minutes. It took hours for us to find Jankom, and even longer to find Rok and Zero, thanks to the Watchers and the energy field guarding them. We still have no idea where Murf is. We just don't have the time. And you heard Yarmie, everyone's underground so they'll be fine. Probably."

Gwyn sneered.

Yarm'orn leaned forward. "I could tell you where to find Murf."

"Yes, please!" cried Rok-Tahk. "And thank you."

Dal turned quickly. "How do you know Murf is?"

Yarm'orn did not answer Dal's question. "And you have more time than you think you do."

"Do we have time for Jankom Pog to eat something?" the Tellarite asked.

"Wait, wait, wait," said Dal. "Explain yourself, Yarmie."

"You and Gwyn were transported near the abandoned generator on Orisi, and Zero and Rok-Tahk were transported near the active one here on Mirios. It sounds like the energy tethers linking the planets to the Dyson sphere acted like magnets, drawing your transporter patterns within a few hours' walk of their planet-side sources."

"So?" Dal was getting impatient.

"So, each of you naturally found your way to the generators. If your friend wasn't beamed down with you to either of the locations on Orisi and Mirios, it would only make sense to assume that he was beamed to the generator on Taresse."

Dal continued to work out the timing. "But even if we do go to Taresse, it could still take hours to find Murf and even longer to shut down the Dyson sphere."

"Not if I told you I could give you the exact coordinates of the generator on Taresse, it wouldn't. Star Killer may have stopped our planets from communicating, but he needed our scientists to be able to share some information to build the Dyson sphere. Only a handful of people know the exact locations of the generators. Only the most senior scientists."

"You were one of those few, weren't you?" Zero asked.

Yarm'orn nodded. "I wasn't always hiding in the shadows. I was once Mirios's minister of science. I would have done anything for Naroan survival. I still will."

Dal approached the Naroan. "So give us the coordinates, Yarmie."

"Not until you promise to stop the sunstar from going supernova."

"There's no time!"

"There is time! There is!"

"How?" asked Rok-Tahk.

"You said the generator you found on Orisi was abandoned and dormant, right?" Yarm'orn began.

"Right," said Gwyn.

"And you just shut down the one here on Mirios."

"I . . ." Dal looked at Rok. "We shut it down. Right."

Yarm'orn stood to his full height. "So that means

the only still-functioning planet-side generator is on Taresse. And, coincidentally, the Taressean bunker that leads to the generator was once used by the Naroans to monitor encrypted alien communications when unidentified ships passed near the system. That system can be reactivated to hack into the Watchers' motherboard and identify the access code that would give you the authority to destroy the Dyson sphere. If you divide into two teams, one can find Murf, shut down the generator, and gain the access code. With none of the three generators actively keeping the Dyson sphere fed, the other team can handle powering down the Dyson sphere and releasing the sunstar from confinement—avoiding the supernova."

Dal tried to take everything in. "That's ... that's a lot. Give us a minute to think."

The *Protostar*'s crew huddled in a corner.

"Jankom Pog says let's get Murf and then get out of here. We don't need to face another Watcher, or another Drednok."

Zero pondered Jankom's position. "I am not sensing any duplicity from Yarm'orn. Just desperation. If we can help the Naroans, do we not have a moral obligation to do so?"

Rok sighed. "I don't know if I can face Drednok again. After what he did—to all of us? I'm scared."

Dal asked, "And what about time travel to gain us a precious few more hours? If we traveled back in time for more hours to do what is needed on Taresse, could we travel forward to come back to right now? Is that even possible, Janeway?"

"Oh, it's possible. In fact, the crew of the USS Enterprise *once went forward to bring two humpback whales to their own time after traveling back to the 1980s to find them. However, the risks of such time travel are great, and the odds of success minute. That mission was led by the only Starfleet cadet to have ever beaten the Kobayashi Maru test."*

"Do you mean James T. Kirk?" asked Zero. "He's famous!"

Dal flinched at the mention of the classic Starfleet test. "We've got our own no-win situation to deal with. How do we rescue Murf and the Naroans before the supernova explodes?"

"You're right, Dal," said Gwyn. "How do we rescue Murf?..."

"And save the Naroans...," added Rok-Tahk.

"And stop Meany Head Star Killer Drednok from killing the sunstar—and all of us in the process?" added Dal.

Zero shook their head. "If I had a brain, it'd be hurting right now."

As they continued to debate the pros and cons of their situation, Dal heard Gwyn mumble. "What?" he asked her.

"I said, what would a true Starfleet officer do?" Gwyn said.

The group paused.

"A true Starfleet officer would help us!" shouted Yarm'orn. "I . . . I can hear everything you're saying. This room has extraordinarily good acoustics."

Dal spoke aloud to the open comm link. "Janeway?"

"Yes, Captain?"

"Five to beam up."

CHAPTER SIXTEEN

*T*he crew gathered on the bridge of the *Protostar*. Now that there was little interference from the Mirios generator, they were able to maintain an open channel with Yarm'orn.

"Now remember," said Yarm'orn from the bridge's viewscreen, "Star Killer knows that this generator is the last one running, so it's sure to be more fortified than the other two. So all one team has to do is get there, destroy the generator, get the access code, and beam out. Before the Watchers get you."

The crew stared at him in disbelief and worry. "The other team has to get to the Dyson sphere and shut down what is unquestionably the most advanced piece of technology ever devised by the Naroan species."

"But we'll have you on comms to help, right?" asked Rok.

"Oh no, my young Brikar friend. The energy coming out of the sunstar, coupled with the shock waves emanating from the fissures, will make communication completely impossible. You'll be on your own!" This pep talk wasn't going as well as Yarm'orn had planned. "But it'll be fine."

"Well, thanks for all that," said Dal, slumping in his chair. "We'll report back. *Protostar* out." The viewscreen disappeared and was replaced by a real-time view of the pulsating Dyson sphere.

Janeway gave a report. "We've taken some hits while you were down on Mirios, but nothing too bad, and not nearly as serious as the initial shock wave that scattered you all over this system. I'm continuing to run diagnostics, but the only real problem is our lack of accurate sensor readings on Taresse. Though we are showing clear signs of the Watchers' unique energy signatures, there's no way to get an accurate count of just how many of them there are or where they are. All I can tell is, as Yarm'orn predicted, there are a lot of them. And there is one additional energy signature. We can surmise, based on what we were able to glean from Drednok's time in—and on—the *Protostar*, that it's Star Killer."

Gwyn's fretwork tingled. "Are you sure?"

"There are too many similarities to think otherwise."

"What about my father?"

"We're unable to detect any life-forms on the planet. Not even Murf."

"But my father could be there?" Gwyn pressed.

"I'd normally say it's a statistical impossibility for your father, or a duplicate, or even a Mirror Universe version of anyone to be anywhere other than where we already know they are, but given that there's another Drednok around, all I can say is that it's . . . improbable."

Gwyn nodded.

Janeway tried to console her. "Cold comfort, I know." Gwyn nodded again.

"Speaking of cold," Dal said, "should we get going down to the ice planet?"

"Not quite an ice planet," corrected Janeway, "but it is well on its way. Temperatures are definitely decreasing, so you and Gwyn better bundle up—it's going to be chilly down there."

She turned to Jankom, Rok, and Zero. "You three, on the other hand, should prepare for much warmer temperatures. The Dyson sphere is maintained by the systems in a control room on the planet's surface. It's going to feel as hot and steamy as New York in August, so be prepared to sweat."

"Where's New York?" asked Rok.

"I think it's near Old York?" offered Zero.

Jankom lifted his arm and took a sniff. "Wherever it is, you should thank Jankom Pog for putting on extra deodorant this morning!"

The crew made their way to the transporter room.

Janeway stood by the controls. "All right. Let's go over your mission orders one last time. Gwyn and Dal, your first priority on Taresse is to find Murf. Once he's safe and in your care, you'll shut down the remaining generator and acquire the access code. Rok-Tahk, Jankom, and Zero, you'll beam over to the Dyson station and monitor the energy flow from the planet. Once the connection is severed, you'll see a significant power fluctuation within the Dyson sphere as it tries to reconnect or reconfigure its last link. All the while, you're to continue to monitor the status of the sunstar and try to extricate it from its containment field. Once Dal and Gwyn send you the access code, you must destroy the Dyson sphere as quickly as possible."

"What's eggstrakate mean?" asked Rok.

Jankom stepped forward. "It means we throw eggs at it until it breaks free!"

"Not exactly, Jankom, but you do need to try to set the sunstar free," said Janeway.

"Okay," said Dal. "We all understand what we need to do. We'll meet you back here soon."

"Very soon, right?" asked Rok.

Dal put on a brave face. "Yeah, Rok. Super soon."

Janeway walked over to the transporter controls. "You'll all be back quicker than a Scalosian running a marathon. Just please be careful."

Dal and Gwyn stepped onto the transporter pad. They looked at Rok one last time. She seemed so sad that all they could do was smile to show that they knew it was all going to work out.

"Energize," said Dal, hoping it would all work out.

CHAPTER SEVENTEEN

"Janeway to Dal."

"I'm here, Janeway."

"Careful. Thanks to Yarm'orn's help, we're able to scan your immediate area. We're picking up lethal defense mechanisms."

Gwyn extended her fretwork. "We don't have time to be careful. Murf is waiting on us."

Dal looked around at the near-frozen landscape. "This planet is colder than the alien graveyard of Rura Penthe." He wrapped his arms around his body to keep warm. He checked his tricorder. Now that they were on-planet, it was showing that they were very close to one life sign.

Gwyn tapped her combadge. "Yarm'orn, can you hear me?"

Back on Mirios, Yarm'orn activated the device the crew had left him. *"Loud and clear, Gwyn."*

"Any advice?"

"Look for access to an underground bunker. The inhabitants of all three planets shared excavation and architectural plans before Star Killer isolated us, so the caves and tunnels systems on Taresse should be just like the ones on Mirios and Orisi. But instead of leading you through a labyrinth like on the other planets, these coordinates should bring you within a few minutes' walk to the generator. I'm sorry I couldn't place you in the tunnel itself, but the closer you get to the generator, the higher the concentration of robots, and it would have been too risky. You could have materialized in a nest of Watchers."

Gwyn kicked away some snow and spotted a set of doors just like the ones they'd fallen next to on Orisi and opened on Mirios. *These are the right coordinates,* she thought.

Dal opened the doors while Gwyn extended her fretwork and shone a light down into the darkness. They couldn't hear anything, including the telltale clicking of Watcher mech, and proceeded, slowly, down the stairs. Despite the ceiling overhead, snow made its way through the doors and onto the stairs, making Dal and Gwyn even more cautious of every footfall. It'd be one thing to come upon a hive of Watchers, but it'd be another thing to draw their attention by falling down a flight of stairs. Dal thought of his Tellarite friend. *Jankom would never let me hear the end of it.*

As they got to the bottom of the stairs, Dal and Gwyn found yet another mural on the walls. It depicted images of humanoids digging a series of tunnels—these tunnels. Legions of diggers excavated and mined beneath the surface of the planet while under the watchful and terrorizing eyes of the Watchers.

"Watchers forcing others to dig and mine? Here, Orisi, Mirios, Tars Lamora. At least they're consistent no matter what planet they're on," said Dal.

Gwyn shook her head. "Or under."

Before the mural ended, its main subject changed from the digging of the tunnel to the construction of what could only be the generator. It was painted much bigger than any of the bipedal figures, and lines radiated out of it, heading up toward a representation of the sunstar.

Gwyn checked her tricorder. "I'm reading a power source—and a life-form—around the next bend."

Working together, they managed to open the entrance to an enormous engine radiating with power. A huge tube extended up through the ceiling.

Dal shielded his eyes. "We found the generator!"

"Yeah. Readings show the energy generated here is tethered directly to the sunstar," observed Gwyn.

"Meeeep!"

"Murf!" Dal and Gwyn ran toward their blue, gelatinous friend. Unlike Rok-Tahk and Zero, Murf seemed to be free to roam the generator room. Murf didn't seem any worse for wear. Gwyn searched the room for clues. It soon became clear that Murf had made his own freedom. She spied shackles, similar to those created by Drednok and Gwyn's father, the Diviner, attached to a stone wall. They were as useless here as they'd been on Tars Lamora. Nothing could hold Murf's elastic and seemingly indestructible body in one place for too long. She held up a shackle and looked at Murf.

"Squeeeeee!" He was very proud of himself.

Dal picked up his pal and swung him around. "How did you get here? How did you get out? Wait, don't answer that." He turned toward the generator. "We have to figure out a way to shut this thing down."

Gwyn started hitting the console with Murf's discarded shackles. "Try hitting it or find something to stab it or somehow break it."

"You're, like, really violent all of a sudden," Dal said to her.

"Our lives are on the line, Dal! Get moving!"

They searched the room but found nothing strong enough to make a dent in the generator's control panel.

Gwyn face-palmed. "Ugh, the one time we could use a Watcher, we don't have one!"

Dal had to agree. He'd spent years trying to avoid the mechanical creatures, and now they were the only thing durable enough to make a difference. "Yeah. The only thing stronger than a Watcher is Murf."

"Murf!" shouted Gwyn and Dal at the same time.

Murf smiled.

CHAPTER EIGHTEEN

Jankom, Rok-Tahk, and Zero beamed from the *Protostar* onto the Dyson station.

"Janeway wasn't kidding," said Jankom. "It's as hot as a Cardassian fire pit in here!"

Rok checked her tricorder for Watcher energy signatures. "Is that better or worse than New York in August?"

"Jankom Pog doesn't know, but Jankom Pog doesn't want to find out. Any Watchers around?"

Rok shook her head. "Nope. That's weird, right?"

Zero checked their tricorder to confirm Rok's report. "Not really. If Drednok, or Star Killer, knew there was only one generator working, he'd want to send as many reinforcements as possible to protect it. This station is self-sufficient, and without much interstellar traffic to contend with, there probably wouldn't be a need to keep any Watchers on guard. Let's find the main control room."

"Rok to Gwyn? Rok to Dal? Janeway? Can anyone hear me?" Rok-Tahk turned to Zero. "They can't hear me."

"I'm not surprised. We're probably too close to the sunstar's radiation for a proper signal to get through. I would imagine the shock waves coming from the fissures are probably sending our transmissions out in erratic and unexpected patterns too."

"Jankom Pog has been called erratic and unexpected," said the Tellarite.

"Yes," said the Medusan. "I expect you have been."

Rok was less worried than she was bored. "So, what do we do now?"

Zero sighed. "I suppose we wait."

Jankom waved at Zero. "Nah—we explore!"

CHAPTER NINETEEN

"**A**re you sure you want to do this, Captain?"

"I'm sure, Janeway."

"*Is Murf sure?*"

Murf looked up at Dal and smiled, inching his way toward the generator. "Yeah, I think he's pretty sure."

"*Well, in that case, good luck. Janeway out.*"

Gwyn crouched down to pet Murf's head. "We're counting on you, Murf. So . . ." She looked at Dal.

"Do your thing?"

"Yeah. Do your thing," finished Gwyn.

With that, Murf bopped and slid along the floor toward the control panel. He looked at it from all angles and perspectives, as if he was trying to figure out which delicious and alien delicacy to sample first in a deep space station food court. He finally settled on a small air duct at the bottom. "Meep!" he squealed, as he slowly worked his way into the vent. Gwyn and Dal waited until they saw his black eyes and purple head pop up in the middle of the containment tube that funneled the energy into the sky. The radiation that would have been deadly for either of them was harmless to Murf. If anything, he seemed to be enjoying himself. Murf circled the inside of the large tube several times, reminding Gwyn of the merry-go-rounds she'd heard the Unwanted talk about back on Tars Lamora. Before being orphaned or kidnapped, they'd spent many happy hours on their home planets visiting parks and community centers, where they rode real or holographic vehicles and creatures around in circles. One boy would always talk about how much fun he'd had holding on to the horn of a mechanical mugato while his younger sister sat beside him in a child-sized shuttle craft. She never stopped the Unwanted from remembering the happy times they'd had before their life on Tars Lamora. It was, she thought, literally the least she could do.

Dal checked his tricorder. "Um, Murf? I hate to rush you, but time's not on our side here. You gotta hurry it up."

"Blrrrrrrrr!"

With that, Murf ducked below their sight line. Moments later, the ground began to shake and the light emanating from the generator began to flicker. Suddenly, everything just stopped and they were thrown into pitch-darkness. Emergency lights illuminated the room, as they watched Murf exit through the same duct he'd entered.

"Good job!" yelled Dal, picking up Murf and spinning him around. "I don't know what you ate—or how you ate it—or, actually, how you're keeping it down—but I'm sure glad you did it!"

CHAPTER TWENTY

Zero, Rok-Tahk, and Jankom Pog walked leisurely around the Dyson station. Rows and rows of computers and workstations led them to believe that the facility was once heavily manned by hundreds of Naroan scientists, technicians, and engineers. The small size of the station belied the massive power it helped contain. Jankom opened an empty storage closet. "Jankom Pog guesses once everything was up and running, they left?"

"Likely. But I can't imagine they had any choice as to when they could come and go. We didn't on Tars Lamora, and if Star Killer is anything like Drednok..." Zero trailed off.

"But Drednok had help. Jankom Pog saw Drednok maybe once a day. And only if Jankom was doing something wrong. But Jankom Pog saw hundreds of Watchers all day every day."

"To make sure you didn't do anything wrong," added Zero. "If the Naroans are gone, then maybe the Watchers aren't needed."

"Maybe this Drednok is different? Maybe he's . . . nicer?" Rok twiddled her fingers hopefully.

Jankom shook his head. "Drednoks are gonna Drednok. Jankom is always right."

"And I can fully admit when I am wrong," said Zero.

"You? When are you ever wrong?" Jankom asked Zero. "Aside from all the times Jankom was right?"

"I'm wrong now," said the Medusan. "Look behind you."

Rok and Jankom turned around slowly. Zero was right. They had been wrong. The Dyson station wasn't devoid of Watchers. They were right there. And there were a lot of them.

The three crewmates ran down the corridor with the clicking-clacking of the Watchers getting louder and louder as they gained on them. Suddenly, the Dyson station shook, throwing the *Protostar*'s crew and the Watchers off their feet and across the hallway. Sirens started to blare out a warning.

"Another shock wave?" asked Zero as they slid across the floor.

Jankom got to his feet and checked his tricorder. "That felt different, and the lights are dimmer now than they were." And as if the station had heard Zero, emergency lights began to flash.

A Watcher approached a screaming Rok-Tahk. Its red eye glowed as brightly as its stinger tail.

"AAAAAAAHHH!" Rok screamed.

Zero got to their feet and ran toward her to help. "Remember, you're not on Tars Lamora anymore, Rok! You're strong!"

"No, no, no! I'm not strong enough!" she cried, hiding her face in her hands, awaiting the inevitable punishment she'd grown used to in the mines.

"That's not true! You're the strongest Brikar I know!"

"I . . . I am?" she sniffed as Zero grew closer and stood between her and the Watcher.

"That wasn't a shock wave," screamed Jankom. "Dal and Gwyn did it—they shut down the generator on Taresse! This Dyson station is running on its own power now!"

Watchers approached the three crewmates.

"You are strong, Rok," Zero continued. "And not just in body, but in mind and heart, too. Trust me. I don't know what it's like to have a body, but I do know that you're much stronger than you think."

Watchers jumped on Zero and Jankom, pinning them to the ground. They fired up their stingers to shock them into unconsciousness.

Rok caught her breath. "I *am* strong. Now get off my friends!" She reached out and grabbed the tail of the Watcher that was closing in on her. She swung it above her head and threw it toward the Watchers attacking Jankom and Zero. Hitting them both with enough force to drive them into the walls, and offline, she stepped over their scattered parts to make sure her friends were okay.

CHAPTER TWENTY-ONE

Dal set Murf back on the ground. "Okay, the generator's shut down. All we need to do now is find the—"

A strange yet familiar voice interrupted the captain. "Find the what?"

"Meany Head?" Dal answered.

Gwyn's neuroflux reflexively readied her fretwork for a fight. "Drednok."

Two pincer-ended tentacles erupted from beneath his cloak. "I prefer Star Killer. In this scenario, at least." The android moved slowly toward Dal. His mechanical legs, like those of the spiderlike Watchers, clicked on the floor's hard surface. "You," he said, moving his left tentacle toward Dal's face. "I don't know you at all." Before Dal could react, Star

Killer's right tentacle swung around and hit him on the side of his head.

Gwyn rushed to Dal. He was unconscious but alive, and she held his head in her hands. She looked up at Star Killer. "Why did you do that? Why?"

Star Killer's red eyes glowed. "Because I wanted a moment alone with you. Progeny."

Gwyn stiffened at hearing what her father called her. "How . . . how do you know . . . ?"

"You have your father's eyes. And his talent for destruction. Thanks to your inherent skills, you have bested all my Watchers. Thus far."

"I didn't do it alone. I had my friends with me." Dal began to stir. Gwyn signaled to him to be quiet and secretly pointed to Murf standing by the console.

"What?" Dal whispered.

"I'll keep Star Killer distracted," Gwyn whispered to Dal, edging in between him and Star Killer. "You and Murf figure out how to get the access code to destroy the Dyson sphere." Dal crawled to the control panel.

"But why—why are you doing this?" Gwyn asked Star Killer, standing tall, doing her very best to hide Dal behind her.

Star Killer looked down on her. "You don't know the whole story, do you? The whole truth? Did your father never tell you about the entire mission to avenge the Vau N'Akat?"

"I don't know what you're talking about," Gwyn answered truthfully.

"You don't, do you?" Star Killer turned from Gwyn toward the door they'd come through. A legion of Watchers began to enter. "I'm not surprised. Your father probably wanted to spare you from the pain of knowing. Lucky for you, I've no qualms with seeing you in pain."

Oh good, thought Dal from the other side of the room. *He's going to start monologuing. That'll give me time to try to figure this all out.*

"Solum's leaders knew there were too many variables in space and time to guarantee any one mission's success. So they sent ships. Solum's bravest ventured back in time to destroy the Federation before it ever made First Contact with the Vau N'Akat. But on my mission . . ." Star Killer stared off in the distance, as if dreamily accessing his memory banks. "Something . . . went wrong. A wormhole opened in the sky. Our navigation and propulsion systems became erratic. Then … nothing." He turned back toward Gwyn and stiffened his posture. "The chances of that kind of spatial anomaly to happen at just the right time … to have that effect on our ship … are statistically impossible. And yet, it was possible. It happened. I awoke on Orisi, alone. My data banks were corrupted. My Vau N'Akat master . . . lost. I was in pieces. I had forgotten … everything.

"But when the Naroan scientists repaired me, I remembered my mission. To save Solum. I saw that I could use their technology to repair the wreckage of my ship and return home. I could harness the power of their sunstar to reopen the wormhole. To return to my time. To try again."

CHAPTER TWENTY-TWO

The Dyson station continued to shake, and the Watchers continued to come. Rok-Tahk, Zero, and Jankom ran down the corridor, searching for weapons or anything to help defend themselves. Nothing. Watchers were coming from all angles, jumping on them, stinging them, but they kept running.

"This way!" shouted Zero, making a sharp right turn down a dimly lit passageway.

Jankom and Rok followed them until they came to the door to the control room. It swished open and they tumbled inside. A Watcher hurled itself into the room with them before the door swished closed. Jankom quickly released his multi-mitt and hit the manual lock, keeping the other Watchers out.

Rok grabbed the Watcher by its stinger tail and ripped it off. She flung the dead mechanical menace to the ground. "And that's for stinging me in the butt all those times on Tars!"

Zero kicked the Watcher's remains away from them. "Well done, Rok!"

"Jankom Pog helped too!"

"Indeed you did, Jankom," said Zero. "Now all we can do is wait. Again."

The station shuddered once more, throwing the crewmates toward the window. Now that they were on the opposite side of the sunstar, they could clearly see the growing wormhole. Each shock wave from the Dyson sphere-covered sunstar seemed to coincide with the wormhole's increasing diameter.

Zero did some mental calculations. They had less than an hour until the sunstar went supernova. *Hurry up, Dal, and get us that access code. We're almost out of time.*

CHAPTER TWENTY-THREE

"**D**id Drednok monologue this much? I don't remember Drednok monologuing this much. Maybe the Naroans didn't put Star Killer all the way back together, if you know what I mean?" Murf did not know what Dal meant.

"I am going home," Star Killer told Gwyn on the other side of the room. "My wormhole device is nearly charged. Then I will attach it to my repaired ship, and use it to return to Solum, to my time, to right what went wrong and erase Starfleet's evildoing. I will save Solum."

"Wiping out an entire planetary system to save Solum isn't the answer!" Gwyn told him.

Star Killer raged. "It is the ONLY answer! And …"

Gwyn waited. "And what?"

"You may come with me."

Gwyn couldn't believe what she was hearing. Go with him? With Star Killer? Drednok? Why would she? How could she ever? But ...

Dal stopped trying to find the access code in the control panel's database. *She can't really be considering going with him?*

Solum. Home, Gwyn thought. She'd never been there. She'd never met another Vau N'Akat other than her father. Surely they weren't all like him? Maybe if she went, she could make a difference. She could show them that Starfleet was not the enemy. Solum didn't have to fall into civil war after Starfleet made First Contact. Solum didn't have to be destroyed. She could save lives.

"You could have ... a family." Star Killer seethed. "Family is all that matters. Your own kind. You have abandoned them to side with our enemy—the Federation. I'm giving you a chance to fix your mistakes, girl. Come with me."

Gwyn saw Dal and Murf looking at her from behind Star Killer. "The Federation is my family now."

"Then you have failed the Vau N'Akat! But fear not. I will succeed in saving them."

CHAPTER TWENTY-FOUR

Hundreds of Watchers clawed at the door to the control room.

Zero surveyed the control panel. "Jankom, I know we cannot shut down the Dyson sphere without the access code, but is there a way to raise shields or do something to give us more time?"

Lights and sirens continued to blare from every possible source. Jankom surveyed the machinery. A complex network of buttons, levers, screens, and switches crowned a series of control panels, all showing rising levels of everything, including and especially danger. "This isn't good."

"What do you mean?" asked Zero.

Jankom pointed to a digital pictogram on a viewscreen. "Look here. Jankom Pog has seen a lot of power, but Jankom Pog has never seen this much power. It may take a while."

The door to the control room began to buckle. The Watchers were almost about to make their way through. Rok threw herself against the door to keep it closed.

"We don't have a while, Jankom," Zero said. "If you can't figure it out quickly, we're all going to die."

"Thanks for not adding any extra pressure, Z."

"Just do your best, Jankom."

CHAPTER TWENTY-FIVE

Star Killer reached for Gwyn and stopped short. Gwyn knew from experience that he, well, Drednok, would do that if he was receiving an urgent message from a Watcher on patrol. It usually had to do with an attempted escape, but this felt different. "You may have succeeded in shutting down the planets' generators, but there is still enough energy from the Dyson sphere to feed the wormhole. It's ninety percent open. By the time I get off-planet and close to it, it will be at ninety-nine percent. And that's more than enough for me to get back home to Solum."

He skirted past the phalanx of Watchers entering the room on his way to his shuttle craft. "Your journey ends here, Progeny. While mine is just beginning."

The door slammed behind him. Watchers creeped over every surface, every inch of wall, getting ready to strike out at Gwyn, Dal, and Murf.

Suddenly, they heard a rumbling coming from behind one of the shelving units. Dal stopped searching the control panel for the access code data. "Another shock wave?"

Similar bunkers, Gwyn remembered. *Same architects.* She rushed to the shelving unit and cleared it of the piles and stacks of tech stored there. Sure enough, she found an air vent—this one much larger—large enough for an adult-sized Naroan to fit through. Before they knew it, the room was filled with a small army of Naroans.

"For Orisi!"

"For Mirios!"

"For Taresse!" they shouted as they emerged carrying long spearlike weapons and joining the *Protostar*'s crew in fighting the Watchers.

Soon enough, the Watchers all lay dismantled and dismembered at their feet.

Once the last of the Watchers was deemed offline, a Naroan approached an out-of-breath Dal. "You must be Captain Dal. My name is Lorn'ess.

Yarm'orn told us what you were doing for us. We thought you could use some help."

Dal shrugged. "Um, yeah. Could have used it a little earlier, but that's okay."

"Where did you come from?" asked Gwyn.

Lorn'ess started entering data into the control panel. "Ever since Star Killer decided he had no further use for us, we retreated to the caves and tunnels beneath our planets. There are . . . there are so few of us left. Nobody on Orisi. Only Yarm'orn remains on Mirios. The remaining Naroans are all here, beneath the surface of Taresse."

"There are so few of you."

"Yes. But we survived. As best we could. And now"—Lorn'ess pointed to a display screen—"we will thrive."

Dal's eyes widened. "Is that the access code?"

"Yes, Captain Dal of Starfleet. It is."

"Well, hit send! Hit send!"

CHAPTER TWENTY-SIX

R ok couldn't hold it anymore. The door exploded into the room. Watchers flooded the space and jumped on top of the *Protostar*'s crew.

"This is it!" yelled Jankom.

Rok screamed in fear. She'd let her friends down, and now they were going to . . .

Suddenly, the Watchers' red eyes went dark. They dropped to their insectoid legs.

We're going to be okay! Rok thought, shoving a Watcher off her and onto the ground.

"They must have accessed the system and shut them down!" Zero cheered.

"And if the Watchers are down, that means Jankom Pog can shut this Dyson sphere down!"

Dal's voice pealed over the sirens and warnings.

"Dal to Rok, Zero, Jankom—can you hear me?"

"Jankom Pog can hear you!"

"Are you all okay? Are you safe?"

Janeway joined the virtual conversation. "My questions, exactly!"

"We're all okay," Jankom answered. "Let's shut down this Dyson sphere!"

Dal recited the access code and Rok punched it into the control panel. And … nothing happened.

"The access code must have been changed," Zero reported. "The Dyson sphere is still active."

"I bet Star Killer changed it when he realized how close we were to stopping him," Gwyn suggested. With no way to shut down the Dyson sphere, the sunstar would go supernova in just a few minutes. Gwyn felt scared and sad, but she refused to dwell on those thoughts. Gwyn was proud of who she was and how hard she had worked to save the Naroans.

Even though they were separated across Taresse, Zero sensed Gwyn's emotions. They were proud of Gwyn too. Proud of each member of the *Protostar* crew. If anyone could figure out another way to save the sunstar from going supernova, it was this crew. "We just have to figure out another way to destroy the Dyson sphere," they said.

"But how?" asked Rok-Tahk. "We don't have any way to destroy it. Just offline Watchers."

"Offline Watchers?" asked Jankom. "That's all we need!" Jankom grabbed the nearest Watcher, the one that had almost been the end of Rok, and affixed his combadge to the bottom of it. "If it worked once, it'll work again!"

Using the same tactics as he'd instructed Dal to employ back on Mirios, Jankom configured the latent power in the combadge to restart the Watcher. Then, taking advantage of his tricorder's connection, the combadge became a wireless remote to control the now-revived killing machine.

"Stand back!" Jankom instructed.

He used the machine's near-indestructible sharp arms to burrow deep within the controls to the Dyson sphere. Once he was confident that the Watcher was as deep into the machine as it was going to get, Jankom used his tricorder to instruct the Watcher to self-destruct.

"Janeway!" shouted Zero. "Three to beam up. Energize . . . now!"

CHAPTER TWENTY-SEVEN

Hologram Janeway greeted Jankom, Rok, and Zero as they materialized on the *Protostar's* transporter pads. Slightly worse for wear, but all in one piece.

"You're all right," she assured them.

Moments later, Murf, Dal, and Gwyn joined them.

Rok extended her wide arms. "Now a group hug?"

"Not yet, Rok," Dal said, running out of the room. "We gotta get to the bridge!"

The crew arrived in time to see Star Killer's ship head toward the wormhole. The Dyson sphere shook. They prepared themselves for a shock wave to hit the *Protostar*, but then realized that the Watcher had just self-destructed, depowering the Dyson sphere.

The wormhole began to close. Quickly.

Zero used the *Protostar*'s navigation systems to calculate Star Killer's trajectory toward the wormhole. "He's not going to make it."

Gwyn stepped toward the viewscreen. "Open a channel to Star Killer's ship, Janeway."

"It's open."

"Drednok. Star Killer. The Dyson sphere is no longer operational. The wormhole is closing." She turned to Zero to confirm, one more time. Zero shook their head no.

Gwyn continued. "I am a child of Solum. I'm telling you that you don't have to do this."

Star Killer's voice flooded the bridge. "You are a wicked child. You have made your home world extinct, and I—"

Suddenly, the transmission cut off.

"What happened?"

"The wormhole completely collapsed," Janeway explained.

"So where is Star Killer?" asked Rok.

"Nowhere. He's trapped in nothingness."

"Oh." Rok looked down. Nobody deserved to be trapped in nothingness.

Later that day, after everyone had taken a long sonic shower, they reconvened on the bridge. Yarm'orn's and Lorn'ess's faces shone at them from the viewscreen.

"Thank you, Captain Dal, for helping us take back our planets," Lorn'ess said.

"Yes. Now that the generators are deactivated and the Dyson sphere is destroyed, there's nothing inhibiting our communications. And the sunstar is shining brightly. Just as it used to." Yarm'orn took a breath. "It's ... it's good to see you again, Lorn'ess."

"The pleasure is mine, Yarm'orn. In fact, the pleasure is ours!" Lorn'ess stepped to the side to reveal a crowd of Naroans. After so many years, they were finally out of the caves and onto the surface of Taresse. "We'll be on Mirios soon, Yarm'orn. You won't be alone for much longer."

Dal sat proudly in his chair. "Glad to be of help, Yarmie. You, too, Lornie! *Protostar* out."

Zero turned in their chair. "Where to now, Captain?"

"Shall we try to find Starfleet?"

Dal slept soundly that night. The next morning, he made an entry into his captain's log.

Captain's Log. Stardate 61185.

Thanks to my *Protostar* crew, the Naroans and their system are saved. I know Gwyn is still struggling with what Star Killer reminded her of. Of Drednok and her father. As for the rest of the crew, including me, I think we're all struggling a little bit with memories too. With what we all went through on Tars Lamora. But I don't think the dangers we're facing here in space make any of us wish we were still there, beaten down into submission. We raise each other up on these missions. And that's what makes us a family. And whatever new challenges await us out here, I know that I'm lucky to have my friends.

Dal walked onto the bridge. Gwyn, Jankom, Zero, Rok-Tahk, and even Murf were at their stations.

"Good morning, Janeway," he said.

Because it *was* a good morning on the Federation starship USS *Protostar*.

DON'T MISS

A DANGEROUS TRADE

ANOTHER ACTION-PACKED NOVEL BASED ON

A NOVEL WRITTEN BY
CASSANDRA ROSE CLARKE

CHAPTER ONE

*J*ankom Pog pulled back the cover of the *Protostar*'s transporter console—and immediately let out a long groan of dismay.

"This doesn't look good!" he said, whipping out the scanning feature on his multi-mitt, which took the place of his right hand. "Jankom Pog will be *very* upset if he gets turned into a targ when he's transporting."

"Jankom? What's wrong?" Gwyndala looked up from her maintenance work to find Jankom frowning down at a panel set in the ship's wall. They were in the transporter room, where the ship's computer could send them down to nearby planets, or even to another ship, on a beam of energy. Assuming they were near any planets or other ships, which at the moment, they weren't.

"One of the phase coils!" Jankom's multi-mitt whirred as he shone a high-powered light on the panel. "It's all worn down." He looked up at Gwyn and gave her a toothy grin. "You don't want to see a transporter malfunction."

"I'm sure I don't." Gwyn set aside her own work and went to stand beside Jankom. While she had some idea of the technology that went into the transporter system on the *Protostar*, she was no engineer, not the way Jankom was, and to her the phase coils looked the same: as shiny and bright as everything else on the ship. "Are you sure it's worn down?"

"Pos-i-tive!" Jankom attacked one of the coils with his multi-mitt, loosening it up so he could show Gwyn the imperfections that he saw. "Look here. Smooth as the bottom on a Melvaran mud flea." Then he popped the coil back into place and turned to Gwyn. "It needs to be replaced."

"Replaced?" Gwyn's eyes went wide as she considered all their options. "I guess we'll have to power up the replicators, then."

"Ah, no can do." Jankom shook his head.

"Replicators can't handle these bad boys." He slapped the phase coil, and it rattled around in its panel. Gwyn felt herself cringe.

"Um, should you—"

"Jankom Pog knows what's too much!" He laughed and smacked it again. "But it will need to be replaced soon. Otherwise, you might wind up with your foot growing out of your head next time we transport you!"

"Wait, you mean we can't use the transporter at all?" Gwyn looked up at the transporter pads in horror.

"Oh, Jankom Pog thinks we can get three or four more transports out of the coil. But then it's blitz-o!" He chuckled.

Before Gwyn could respond, a familiar face—and equally familiar shock of gray and white hair—popped into the transport room. Dal R'El strolled in with a cool air, making a show of examining the space. Gwyn resisted the urge to roll her eyes.

"I thought you were monitoring our flight trajectory," Gwyn said.

"I was," Dal replied as he plopped down in the transporter station chair. "But then I remembered

I needed to check on my favorite engineer."

"Well, you've got great timing," Gwyn said with a smile. "Because Jankom found a problem."

Dal's only reaction, however, was to give an easy grin and straighten his spine. He ran a hand through his hair. "The captain's ready to hear it."

Jankom immediately began laying out the problem of the transporter phase coil.

"So we replicate it," Dal said.

"Too late," Gwyn said. "I already suggested that."

"The replicator can't solve all our problems!" Jankom let out a loud, exasperated sigh. "Jankom Pog has spent a lot of time studying this transporter. Look." He popped the phase coil out of place again and held it up to the light. "See those squiggles there? In the metal? Those have to be programmed by hand. Replicator can't do it." He put the phase coil back and slid the cover in place.

"So what are you saying?" Dal asked. "What are we going to do? We're going to need to use the transporter eventually!"

Jankom crossed his arms over his chest and looked at Dal straight on. "We need to buy a new phase coil."

"Buy?" Gwyn blinked. "With what currency?"

"Yeah," said Dal. "We lost all our chimerium, remember?" He threw his hands up in the air as he slumped back dramatically in his chair. "We're broke!"

Gwyn looked over at Jankom, who shrugged.

"We should call in the others," she said. "Maybe Janeway knows of a secret stash of chimerium on the ship?"

"Doubtful," Dal muttered, but he still tapped on his combadge. "Crew, this is your captain speaking. I need everyone to meet me in the transporter room. We've got a problem." Then he dropped his hand into his lap and beamed triumphantly at Gwyn.

"You didn't have to make it sound quite so dramatic, you know."

"Our transporter is busted!" Dal said. "I'd say that's an emergency."

"Not busted," Jankom interjected. "We just need to buy a new part."

"But we don't have any way to do that," Dal said. "Which is why—"

Voices echoed down the corridor: the bright, cheerful chatter of Rok-Tahk and the calm, soothing lilt of Zero. A second later, Rok-Tahk burst in through the doorway, Murf cradled in her arms.

"What'd you bring him for?" Dal asked.

"You said everyone!" Rok-Tahk responded, and Murf cooed and rubbed his head against her chest. She giggled.

"And you said there was a problem." Zero drifted in after Rok-Tahk. Where Rok-Tahk was strong and solid, her body like carved granite, Zero was light and compact, their true form contained in a makeshift containment suit. "It sounded serious, in fact."

"You forgot to call Janeway," Gwyn said, before raising her voice slightly and speaking to the ship. "Janeway! We might need your help."

Instantly, a human woman materialized next to the chair where Dal was still sitting. It was Janeway, the ship's holographic training adviser.

"Help?" Janeway raised an eyebrow. "And here I thought the six of you had the running of the ship down."

Dal rolled his eyes. "Well, we ran into a problem."

"Just tell us what it is!" Rok-Tahk cried. Murf wriggled out of her arms and made his way around the perimeter of the room, investigating the equipment.

"Don't let him eat anything," Dal said. "Otherwise we're going to need to dig up even more chimerium."

"Chimerium!" Janeway cried. "What do you need chimerium for?"

"Jankom, tell 'em."

Dal sighed, and Jankom launched once again into the issue of the transporter's worn-down phase coil.

"That does sound like quite the pickle," Janeway said when he was done.

"Agreed." Dal sat up, shaking back his hair. "We were hoping you'd know where there's a secret stash of chimerium on the ship."

Janeway laughed. "I'm afraid there's no such thing. As crew, it'll be your job to find a workable solution."

Dal groaned, throwing his back against the chair. "Greeeeeeeeat," he said. "What are we going to do?"

The crew exchanged glances with one another, concern flickering across their features.

"Maybe we could ask someone for it," Rok-Tahk said. "Like, another ship? Maybe they'd let us borrow one of their coils."

Jankom laughed. "They'll need it for their own transporter!"

"But what if they have a spare?"

"It's possible, but unlikely," Janeway said. "And this far into the Delta Quadrant, we don't tend to run across other ships that frequently either."

"Janeway has a point." Dal rubbed his chin, considering their options. "But we can get to a market easily enough. We just need money." He frowned, settling deeper into his thoughts. The woman who raised him, a Ferengi named Nandi, had taught him all about the importance of money. Of course, that had led to her selling him to the Diviner, who forced him to work in the Tars Lamora mines, so maybe her perspectives weren't entirely trustworthy. He certainly wasn't going to sell any of his crew—to the Diviner or anyone else—just to replace a phase coil. But if they had something else—

Dal snapped his fingers and sat up in his chair. "I've got it!"

ROBB PEARLMAN is a pop culturalist, publishing professional, and #1 *New York Times* bestselling author of more than sixty books, including *Fun with Kirk and Spock*, *The Wit and Wisdom of Star Trek*, *Star Trek: My First Book of Colors*, *Star Trek: The Girl Who Made the Stars*, *The Star Trek Book of Friendship*, *Starfleet Is...*, *Star Trek Discovery: The Book of Grudge*, *Search for Spock*, *Body by Starfleet*, and *Redshirt's Little Book of Doom*. He is also a Trekspert who appears at pop culture events and conventions across the country. He lives in New Jersey and summers on Vulcan.